Zorgoochi Intergalactic Pizza

DELIVERY
OF
DOOM

ZORGOOCHI

Solaro

Founder of Zorgoochi Intergalactic Pizza

Developed famous Zorgoochi Pizza Toss

Discovered the Golden Anchovy

Vulcanelli

Invented the first volcano-powered pizza oven

Founder of the Pizza Pyramid

Forza

Developed the first four-dimensional pizza

A champion wild mushroom wrestler

Pomodoro

Inventor of a pizza able to travel safely at the speed of sound

Created geometrically perfect meatballs

FAMILY LINEAGE

Infinito

Inventor of the Pizza Ball

Developed a pizza box strong enough to withstand extreme G-forces

Tomino

Developed a mathematical formula to create eight precisely identical slices in every pizza

Perfected microscopic pizza

Geo

Inventor of the zero-gravity pizza delivery box

Developed an award-winning pneumatic olive pitter

Illuminato

Geo's son, a pizza delivery boy who's the sole protector of the Zorgoochi Intergalactic Pizza family recipe

Zorgoochi Intergalactic Pizza

DELIVERY

OF

DOOM

Written and illustrated by

DAN YACCARINO

[handwritten inscription: For John and Marele! — signature]

Feiwel and Friends   New York

A FEIWEL AND FRIENDS BOOK
An Imprint of Macmillan

Library of Congress Cataloging-in-Publication Data Available

ISBN: 978-1-250-00844-2 (hardcover) / 978-1-250-00845-9 (ebook)

Book design by Anna Booth

Feiwel and Friends logo designed by Filomena Tuosto

First Edition: 2014

10 9 8 7 6 5 4 3 2 1

mackids.com

For Sue.
Finally.

More Than One Thousand Years from Today

EARLY MORNING

Deep in the Mezzaluna Galaxy, in one of its lesser spiral arms, on a tiny gray planet called Industro12, seven-year-old Luno Zorgoochi placed his small hand in his father's as they walked through the herb garden behind the family pizzeria. It was Luno's favorite place to be because it was so different from the rest of Industro12. Quiet and lush, with a maze of babbling brooks running through it, it was the only spot on the entire planet that wasn't covered in concrete, metal, or was the site of a factory belching smoke.

They strolled past rows of oregano, basil, and Erba Zorgoochus, the secret herb that made Zorgoochi

Intergalactic Pizza the tastiest in the entire Mezzaluna Galaxy and possibly the entire universe.

At least that's what Luno's father, Geo, believed.

"You know, son," Geo said, looking down at Luno as they walked into the greenhouse, past basketball-size tomatoes and zucchini as long as canoes, "your great-great-great-great-great-grandfather Solaro planted the garden and built this greenhouse about two hundred years ago."

Luno looked down as his space boots walked over the ornate mosaic imbedded in the tile floor, then squinted up at the sun streaming through the greenhouse's geometric latticework. He nodded and smiled. Sure, his father had already told him a million times, but Luno didn't mind hearing it again. And again and again and again. He *liked* listening to his father tell him how Solaro got up every morning before dawn to make the whitest, smoothest, lightest dough along with a big pot of his ancestor Nonna Prima's secret tomato sauce recipe that Colono, one of his forefathers from the remote past took with him as he escaped Earth before it was destroyed. Since then it was passed down from generation to generation.

Solaro also spent years perfecting the Zorgoochi Pizza Toss, his own special way of spinning dough in the air, which made his pizza crust crunchy on the outside, soft on the inside, and like no other pizza in the galaxy.

Solaro was known for his famously keen sense of smell. Not only did he know if a pizza was done just by its aroma, but he could also smell a pizza three light-years away and identify its toppings.

When Solaro was a young man, he left home for Planet Formaggio to train with the legendary Mozzarella Monks, a band of devout cheese artisans, who taught him the ancient secrets of how to make the

3

finest mozzarella in the universe. With his training complete, Solaro returned home to Industro12, opened a little pizzeria, and called it Zorgoochi Intergalactic Pizza. Soon word spread throughout the galaxy about Solaro's perfect pizza and sentient beings of all kinds came to have a slice.

Because he only used the freshest ingredients, Solaro grew his own vegetables, ground his own wheat, and fished for his very own anchovies for his pizzas. One day while fishing in the Sea of Tranquility, he spotted an anchovy that was different from any one he'd ever seen.

"Why was it *different*, Daddy?" Luno asked, even though he already knew the answer.

"Because it was golden"—his father bent down and leaned in close, his eyes bright—"and it *glowed*."

Even though he had heard it many times before, Luno's eyes grew wide as his father described what happened next.

"Solaro placed his palms in the water and the little fish swam right to him," said Geo. "And when he touched it, Solaro had a mystical vision."

As with every telling, Luno gasped, even though he still didn't know exactly what a "mystical vision" *was*, but knew it must've been pretty important.

"That anchovy reached deep down into Solaro's soul and showed him his life's true purpose: to make the greatest pizza in the universe!" Geo looked around, and then whispered, "One with Everything."

Luno listened agape as his father recounted what *his* father told *him* and *his* father told *him* and so on: Not only did the Golden Anchovy reveal Solaro's life's mission, but it also guided and protected him as he fulfilled his vision.

This was also where the ancient phrase "hold the anchovies" actually came from. It originally started off as "hold the Anchovy," meaning the *Golden Anchovy*, as a kindly greeting from one pizzeria owner to another, but over the centuries the uninitiated unknowingly changed the singular into plural.

Solaro kept the Golden Anchovy in a flask tucked safely inside his space suit, close to his heart when he traveled to the farthest reaches of the galaxy on his quest to gather the ingredients for this perfect pizza.

Finally, after many years, the One with Everything was complete. He decided to cut it into three slices to resemble a peace symbol.

The first thing Solaro did was brave a dangerous space battlefield to deliver slices to each side. With the soldiers' stomachs full of pizza and their hearts now full of love, the

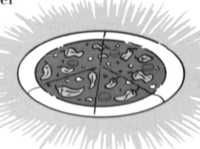

Thousand-Year Space War ended. There was peace in the galaxy at last!

Keeping the Golden Anchovy close, Solaro delivered his One with Everything to heal the sick, raise the dead, and feed thousands with the single pie. There was always enough since the slices regenerated themselves.

"Once word got out about the Golden Anchovy," said Geo, "everyone wanted it, but there was one who wanted it most of all."

"Vlactron," Luno whispered with a mix of fear and scorn.

"That's *right*." His father nodded.

"Did he want to make a pizza, *too*, Daddy?" Luno asked.

Luno's father smiled and sat on an overturned tomato basket, then pulled another over and patted it for Luno to sit down.

"No, son, he *didn't*," Geo said. "He wanted the Golden Anchovy for its *power*. Your great-great-great-great-great-grandfather, he used it to help *others*, but Vlactron wanted to use it for *himself*. And *that's* the difference between a good guy and a bad guy."

Solaro hid the Golden Anchovy, well knowing that Vlactron would do anything to get his claws on it. He hid it so well, even his son and grandsons, great and otherwise, couldn't find it. Maybe he was just trying to protect them from Vlactron. Maybe he was waiting for the right Zorgoochi to find it at the right time.

Years later, Solaro handed down his pizzeria to his son, Vulcanelli, the mechanical genius who built the kitchen's volcano-powered ovens. Vulcanelli then handed the pizzeria to *his* son, Infinito, who created a pizza box so strong it could withstand the most extreme gravitational pressure. And then *he* handed it to *his* son, Tomino, who calculated the mathematical formula for every pizza to be sliced into eight identical pieces, so there would be no arguments about who got a bigger slice, then to Forza, who designed the first four-dimensional pizza, then Pomodoro, who created a pizza that could travel at the speed of sound without disintegrating, and finally to Luno's dad, Geo, who invented a zero-gravity delivery box, so the pizza wouldn't get stuck to the bottom or the top.

Along with the family's secret tomato sauce recipe and the famous Zorgoochi Pizza Toss, Zorgoochi Intergalactic Pizza was handed down from father to son, decade after decade, improving the pizzeria and perfecting the pizza with each generation.

"Then it was handed down to *me* from *my* father," Luno's dad said with a twinkle in his eye. "And someday, Zorgoochi Intergalactic Pizza will be handed down to *you*."

They walked in silence, until Luno stopped and looked up.

"Is the Golden Anchovy for *real*, Daddy?" he asked suspiciously, cocking his head.

"Of *course* it's for real!" Geo Zorgoochi smiled, then knelt down and held Luno's tiny shoulders between his big calloused hands. "Maybe *you'll* be the one to find it! Do you remember the little rhyme I taught you?"

Luno nodded, then they both recited:

"When you touch the Golden Fish
You fulfill your truest wish.
It will guide and keep you free from harm
In Mezzaluna's spiral arm.
And when your vision has been done
Give it to a special one.
Or release it into the starry stream
For others to realize their dream.
But if you steal it, you hereby
Cause the Golden Anchovy to die."

"Geo!"

The back door swung open and Mom appeared.

"How many times have I told you not to fill Luno's head with that silly anchovy nonsense," Luno's mother, Connie, scolded.

"*Uffa!* Gimme a *break*, Connie. I'm only having a

little fun with the kid," said Geo. "Besides, *my* father told *me* the same thing."

"And those stories about that Vlactron character have been giving him nightmares!" Connie shouted, and then turned to Luno. "Daddy's just making those things up, *aren't* you, Geo?"

Geo reluctantly nodded, but when she turned away, he gave Luno a secret wink.

"Now come into the kitchen, sweetheart," Connie said to Luno. "You look hungry."

As he bit into a hot slice of pizza, Luno thought about the Golden Anchovy and the day *he* would take over the pizzeria, and learn the famous Zorgoochi Pizza Toss just like his dad and every other Zorgoochi before him.

And maybe even be the one to find the Golden Anchovy.

PART 1

CHAPTER ONE

Six Years Later

"Vake *up*, boy!" Roog shouted, smacking Luno on the head with his metal claw as he tried to toss pizza dough in the air.

"No good enough!" barked Roog. "*Again!*"

Just like every morning, Luno tried to perfect the famous Zorgoochi Pizza Toss, and just like every morning, it was far from perfect. At least *this* time it didn't stick to the ceiling.

"I have trained all Zorgoochi for last two hundred year," barked Roog, "and you are vorst of all! *Again!*"

Even though he could barely feel his arms, Luno tried again.

And again and again and again and *again.*

Luno began to think he *wasn't* a Zorgoochi after all. Maybe there was a mix-up at the hospital and the *real* Luno Zorgoochi went home with another family and was out there somewhere tossing pizza dough perfectly.

And what would *Dad* think? How could Luno ever take over Zorgoochi Intergalactic Pizza with a crummy pizza toss?

In his zeal to master the Zorgoochi Pizza Toss, Luno went as far as to invent a pair of Memory Gloves, which he had his father wear when he tossed pizza dough. Once the microscopic circuitry recorded the movements of Geo's nimble fingers, then all Luno had to do was slip them on and the gloves would do all the work.

Unfortunately, the Memory Gloves malfunctioned and tried to strangle Luno.

"Your fazzer, he master Zorgoochi Pizza Toss vhen he vas *ten!*" Roog growled. "You cannot take over pizzeria unlezz you do Toss *perfek!*"

Roog shook his head in disgust. He had helped train every generation of Luno's family to make pizza since Solaro hired him, and from then on, he sort of came with the place. Luno had no idea how old Roog was, where he came from, or anything else about him other than he had a prosthetic metal claw from being wounded in the Great Pizza War of Deep Dish vs. Thin Crust, and liked to yell at him.

Every morning before school, Roog trained Luno in the basics of pizza making, including the dozens of hand signals, like baseball catchers used, to identify the different kinds of pizzas, as well as how to hold your breath underwater long enough to pick a bushel of Sea Garlic in the kitchen tank without drowning.

Every day after school Luno wrestled Cosmic Calamari, deflated Plutonian Pufferfish, and shucked giant snapping Space Clams, which was bad enough, but he also had a seafood allergy and had to wear a protective suit to handle them or he'd swell up like one of those Pufferfish he popped every day. However, Luno *still* wasn't entirely sure how dodging flying pizza cutters, walking across hot coals, or taking apart and reassembling a pizza oven blindfolded had anything to do with making pizza.

"You call dis meatball, boy?" shouted Roog as he pelted Luno with meatballs with microscopic imperfections. "Your grandfazzer Pomodoro, he made perfek meatball no vun could bear eet, they ver so beautiful! *Again!*"

As Luno attempted to make perfect spheres of ground meat, he daydreamed about what it would be like to play sports, be in the school band, or just not have to work at his parent's pizzeria every morning and afternoon, and now that school was over, for the entire summer. But his reverie was cut short by a strange feeling on his leg.

Luno looked down and his spine froze. A Saturnian Sausage with a hungry look in its eye was slithering up his pant leg!

"Vhat are *doing*, zilly boy?" Roog bellowed. "Dat zausage iz about to keel you! Dere is no time to be afraid!"

Luno pulled the sausage off and whipped it into a massive bubbling pot of Zorgoochi special tomato sauce.

"Maybe I forget to lock cage, eh?" Roog chuckled. "It vas accident, I tink."

Roog seemed to have lots of "accidents," but only when no one else other than Luno was around. No matter how many times Luno complained, his parents

never believed him. Once, Roog "accidentally" knocked Luno into the laundry dryer and he was left spinning for an hour until his mother discovered him tangled up with the aprons. Another time, Roog "absentmindedly" locked him in the walk-in cryogenic freezer for two days. Luno had to keep moving or he would've been frozen solid. It took a whole week for his eyebrows to defrost.

Luno had the sneaking suspicion that Roog was trying to kill him.

One thing Roog *didn't* yell at Luno about was his sense of smell. In fact, Luno was his school's Smelling Bee champ five years in a row.

Roog threw Luno into a chair and blindfolded him. Then he passed different herbs under his nose.

"Basil!" Luno said. "Parsley, sage, cayenne pepper—ah-*choo*!"

Then Roog waved another leaf under Luno's nose.

"Erba Zorgoochus." Luno smiled.

Roog pulled the blindfold off.

"Not bad. You inherited nose from great-great-great-great-great-grandfazzer Solaro," Roog grunted. "A nose like his only happens every six generation. You are lucky, boy."

When Luno was younger and Roog told him that, he thought Roog only meant that he had a nose that was as super-sensitive as Solaro's, but now that he was thirteen, it was starting to look like he also inherited a nose as *big* as his ancestor's.

It also had its drawbacks. No matter how hard they

Cayenne Pepper

Sage

tried, his parents were never able to successfully throw him a surprise birthday party because he could always smell the cake before he saw it.

"Okay, boy," Roog said. "Time to make de pizza."

Erba Zorgoochus

Basil

Parsley

CHAPTER TWO

Surprise (But Not the Good Kind)!

Luno sat on an overturned tomato basket and breathed in the dozens of aromas in the garden behind the pizzeria. It still was his favorite place to be—and to get away from Roog. He closed his eyes and let the rays of the three suns warm his face as he leaned against the greenhouse.

"Luno!" his father barked. Luno wheeled around with a start and saw his parents ambling toward him.

"We need to talk to you about something," said Geo.

The last time his father said that, he had to start working in the kitchen every day before *and* after school *and* on weekends *and* in the summer.

"I still don't think it's a good idea," Connie said, "but your father thinks you're ready."

"For *what*?" Luno asked, his stomach flip-flopping.

"To be Zorgoochi Intergalactic Pizza's new delivery boy," said Geo.

Luno suddenly forgot how to blink.

"*So?*" Geo asked hopefully. "What do you say, son?"

Luno didn't know *what* to say. Sure, he was happy about not spending another summer down in the hot kitchen with Roog, wrestling angry sausages, getting shocked by electric olives, or being bitten by wild mushrooms. But driving around the galaxy delivering pizzas—*all by himself?*

Luno's parents never allowed him to leave the planet, but he always dreamed of going out into the cosmos ever since he turned twelve and got his galactic driver's license. He'd been begging his parents to let him drive on his own and now it was actually *happening*!

GULP!

Luno was about to ask why William10, the

Zorgoochi's outdated robot delivery autopilot, couldn't do the job, but then he remembered. Sporting a major dent in his side, most likely from a particularly dangerous delivery, William10 was so old and banged-up, they retired him to Rusty Acres on Planet Rur, a planet for old robots, when he could no longer control his radioactive gas emissions. The Zorgoochis couldn't afford another robot, so not only did his father make the pizzas, he *delivered* them, too, which was probably why he was so tired and grumpy all the time.

Luno realized he finally *did* get what he wanted—but only *sort of.* He felt his heart beat faster and didn't know whether it was because he was happy or scared . . . or *both.*

Zooming around the galaxy *could* be fun, but he worried he might get lost, not get paid, or, even worse, get *eaten* by an unhappy customer! Luno even heard that his great-great-great-uncle Tempo went out on a delivery and *never came back!*

He noticed his mom's anxious expression, but his

father just looked kind of weary. The twinkle in his eye had dulled just about the time Quantum Pizza, Mezzaluna Galaxy's largest pizza chain, opened a few years ago.

All his life, Luno heard over and over how hard his ancestors had worked to keep Solaro's dream alive. Luno also knew that now with Quantum Pizza in their galaxy, his family's little pizzeria had big competition, especially since Quantum had been intercepting Zorgoochi's pizza orders and delivering them first. Zorgoochi couldn't beat Quantum's drive-thru/fly-thru windows, edible delivery boxes, and free gravity with every purchase, either. Quantum even started installing APMs (automatic pizza machines) everywhere, so anyone could have pizza anytime they wanted. Nobody seemed to mind that it just didn't taste very good.

A few months ago, Quantum had taken so much business away from Zorgoochi Intergalactic Pizza that his dad couldn't pay the monthly gravity bill. Everything floated around the pizzeria until he got enough money together to pay it. Luno knew they would have to work even harder to keep the family business going and his parents really needed his help. He couldn't let them down.

Besides, whether he liked it or not, Luno knew it was time he joined the proud Zorgoochi line. Every ancestor had contributed *something* to Zorgoochi

Intergalactic Pizza. But how could he even come close to achieving something like the famous String Cheese Theory of his great-great-great-aunt Genia, the physicist? Or his great-great-great-grandfather Infinito's invention of the Pizza Ball, which you used to play spaceball but, afterward, ate it.

But what would *Luno*'s contribution be? When he wasn't in the kitchen, Luno spent most of his time trying to come up with an idea for the pizzeria that would bring the sparkle back to his father's eyes, but nothing he ever created made his father happy—or actually *worked*. The teleportation device that delivered pizza using radio waves, the liquid pizza that filled you up and quenched your thirst at the same time, and the pizza seed that could be planted and harvested—*all disasters.*

Luno even managed to screw up something as simple as a pizza bagel and accidentally made a pizza *beagle*, which bit him.

He wasn't the greatest speller.

Other times Luno just wanted to be an ordinary spacekid, not one who worked in his family business. Maybe he *didn't* want to take over the pizzeria some-day and toss pizza dough for the rest of his life. Maybe he wanted to do something else.

And *that's* where he always got stuck. What did he truly want to do? Luno could never figure that part out. All he knew was pizza. His father said tomato sauce ran through the Zorgoochi veins.

In school, when other kids were voted Most Likely

to Succeed or Most Likely to Be the Most Famous Life-Form in Five Dimensions, Luno was voted Most Likely to Make Pizza for the Rest of His Life.

He knew he couldn't fight it. It was his destiny.

His father looked at him with tired eyes, hoping Luno would agree to be Zorgoochi Intergalactic Pizza's new delivery boy.

"So?" Geo asked. "What do you say, son?"

"Um, okay," Luno said. "I guess so."

CHAPTER THREE

*Quite Preposterous, Highly Illogical,
and Utterly Unscientific*

No sooner had Connie's tears, hugs, and kisses stopped than Geo announced that Luno would be making his first deliveries—*in ten minutes!*

Luno swallowed hard and before he could set off to his room to get dressed, Geo placed a hand on his shoulder.

"*Grazie,* son," he said with weary relief. "Thank you." But then he looked around, making sure Connie was out of earshot.

"Y'know, this isn't going to be like those stories about Solaro I used to tell you when you were a little boy," Geo said, referring to all the tales he had told him about his great-great-great-great-great-grandfather and the Golden Anchovy, which Luno eventually found out had all been made up by his father.

"That was for fun. This is for *real*," Geo said, putting his hand on Luno's shoulder. "We need you—*Zorgoochi Intergalactic Pizza* needs you to be grown up and responsible now. *Capish?*"

"I understand," said Luno.

"It can get dangerous out there and I want you to promise you'll be *careful*," Geo said.

Luno looked at his feet and nodded.

"Your *mother*," Geo said awkwardly, "she—y'know—*worries* about you."

"It's okay, Dad," Luno replied. "I-I won't let you down."

As Luno walked down the hallway toward his room, the door sensed his approach and gave a soft hiss as it rose up from the floor. He walked in. As usual, Clive was sitting at Luno's desk tinkering with one of his gadgets.

Earlier in the semester, Luno had an assignment for Galactic Biology class to shoot an ordinary, everyday piece of organic matter full of gamma rays and record the results. He chose a bulb of garlic from the kitchen, thinking he'd create a new taste sensation for his dad's pizzas, but all he ended up with was a vegetable-based know-it-all.

Luno had no idea where this oversize garlicky genius got the lab coat and tie.

"Good afternoon, Mr. Zorgoochi," Clive said.

"Will you *please* stop calling me *Mr. Zorgoochi?*" Luno asked for the millionth time since Clive sprouted a few months ago.

"Certainly, Mr. Zorgoochi," replied Clive, not looking up, as he pecked away at a small handheld device he'd assembled from six pop bottle caps, a discarded atomic generator, and a pizza cutter.

It seemed to Luno that Clive's favorite things to do were building gadgets, studying the universe, and annoying him, but he had to admit Clive was good to have around for help with Molecular Mathematics homework.

Besides, for a super-intelligent gamma-ray-infused mutant bulb of garlic, Clive wasn't so bad.

Luno was Clive's best friend, if he actually had one. Clive's second-best friend was a mold spore he kept in a petri dish in the back of the closet.

Clive was actually Luno's second attempt at his Galactic Science class homework. His first was shooting an eggplant full of gamma rays, which turned out to be a catastrophe. It sprouted legs and ran around the kitchen eating everything in sight, including Luno's pet pizza beagle. It was the first time in the universe someone's homework ate their dog.

Suddenly, the room began to shake.

CLUNK! CLANK! *CLUNK!*

The walls shuddered from the approach of heavy metallic footsteps. It could only be one person. Well, it wasn't exactly a *person*; it was *Chooch*.

Before the door panel could rise, all 32 galactic tons of him burst right through it.

"Oops," he squeaked. "I keep forgetting to wait for the door to open *first*. Sorry, Luno."

Last spring break, when Luno had to work in the kitchen while other kids were zooming around the galaxy having way more fun than him, Connie suggested he make a new friend, so Luno dragged in an old pizza oven from the junkyard across the street and some electronics destined for recycling, got out his toolbox, and did just that. Unfortunately, Luno had a steady C- average in robotics and his new friend didn't exactly turn out the way he'd hoped.

C.H.O.O.C.H. (Computerized Hydrogen-Operated Oscillating Cybernetic Humanoid) was a 32-galactic-ton whiney pizza oven, who loved kittens, bright colors, and ice cream, but was afraid of clowns, broccoli, and being left alone in the dark. It was as if Luno had an incredibly accident-prone crybaby little brother who was about ten thousand times bigger than him and who followed him everywhere. Luno sort of got used to him and decided not to disassemble him—*for now.*

"I'm so *clumsy!*" Chooch began to blubber.

"I know you didn't mean to smash the door"—Luno sighed—"*again*," patting him on the back as brake fluid poured out of Chooch's eyes and all over the floor. "It was just an accident."

"You're *right*, Luno," sniffed Chooch, "I shouldn't cry over chilled milk."

"Hmmm," said Clive. "It appears that Chooch has sprung a leak."

"He's *crying*, Clive," said Luno. "You do it when your feelings get hurt."

"Please define 'feelings,' Mr. Zorgoochi," said Clive, eagerly taking notes.

For someone who's IQ was about 500 times higher than any human's, Clive sure didn't know a lot. Before Luno could explain, he heard a shout from the kitchen.

"Hey, Luno!" Geo called. "You've got deliveries! *Andiamo!* Get a move on!"

Luno mopped up Chooch's tears, changed his clothes, and then ducked through the broken door.

Moments later, Luno was climbing the stairs to the roof where the pizza delivery pod was parked, when Roog appeared, blocking his way.

"Zo," Roog grunted. "I hear you now make deliwery, eh, boy?"

"Yes, I now make delivery," Luno said suspiciously, waiting for Roog to give him a live scorpion sandwich or dangle him out the window by his boots and tell him it was part of his pizza training.

"De universe, she big place, ya? Lots of danger for leetle boy like you," Roog said, placing his metal claw on Luno's shoulder and looking him in the eye. "Be careful, Luno."

Luno didn't know what to do. It was the nicest thing Roog had ever said to him. He choked out "thanks" and squeezed past him.

Luno pushed open the door and saw his father and Chooch waiting for him. The rickety Zorgoochi Pizza delivery pod's engine was rattling away as if it was going to fall apart any moment, which it had a habit of doing.

Connie fussed with his hair and Geo awkwardly patted him on the back, giving Luno a weary smile.

"Ah, I remember *my* first delivery," Geo said with a sigh. "It was to a planet of tree creatures. They paid me in acorns. Boy, was my old man unhappy about *that!*"

Then Geo announced that the first delivery was to Inferno9, a fire planet.

Luno froze. *A fire planet?* He was actually hoping his first delivery would be to someplace *good* like Planet Jupico, where the biggest ice cream factory in the galaxy was, or Planet Ludum, where they designed electro-brain games like Asteroid Dodger. Now *that* would be cool. In fact, *anything* would be cooler than a fire planet. Most things were.

"This is gonna be so much *fun*, Luno!" Chooch squealed, hopping from one foot to the other with excitement . . . or maybe he just needed an oil change.

Luno turned to his parents. Not wanting to hurt Chooch's feelings, he just gave them a look. They knew Luno was silently asking if he had to take Chooch on the delivery.

"Chooch'll keep the pizzas hot while you drive," Geo said, and then opened the oven in Chooch's chest to show Luno, giving him a blast of heat and scorching his eyebrows. "*Brutto Malo!*" he cursed, but quickly recovered.

"Geo!" Connie scolded. "Watch your language!"

"Aaah!" Geo sniffed one of the pizzas with pride. "A large Zorgoochi super-spicy pizza with extra hot peppers!"

"Large?" Clive asked, approaching them. "As compared with *what*?"

Luno rolled his eyes. *There he goes again.*

"Something can only be 'large' if it is compared with something *smaller*," Clive explained.

Connie informed Luno that Clive would be going on the delivery, too.

"He's been alphabetizing the pizza toppings again and it's driving your father crazy. *You* made him; he's *your* responsibility."

Luno sighed and loaded Clive and Chooch into the pod and climbed in after them.

Luno was about to go out into the galaxy *all alone*, except for having Clive and Chooch with him, which was roughly the same thing, possibly *worse*. Maybe Roog was right; the universe *was* full of danger, but there was no turning back now.

Luno swallowed hard.

Before he closed the hatch, he gave his parents a quick wave and attempted a smile, trying to look as if everything was under control, but Geo recognized Luno's anxious expression.

"You already know what to do, son," he said. "Now *do* it."

Luno wasn't sure if he really *did* know what to do, but nodded anyway.

He closed the hatch and dropped himself into the driver's seat.

"Ladies and gentlemen," said Chooch, "please make sure your seat back and folding trays are in their full, upright position."

Luno sighed, regretting having used a salvaged circuit board from a junked passenger cruiser for Chooch's voice system. He then took a deep breath and tried to remember everything he learned in Interstellar Driver's Ed.

"Mr. Zorgoochi?" asked Clive, as he secured his seat belt. "Have you ever operated this vehicle?"

"No," said Luno.

"Have you ever left the planet?" asked Clive.

"No," said Luno.

"Have you ever delivered a pizza?" asked Clive.

"No," said Luno.

"Well, Mr. Zorgoochi," said Clive, "I find this endeavor quite preposterous, highly illogical, and utterly unscientific."

Luno tried to ignore the obvious and set the coordinates for Inferno9.

"I have to go to the bathroom," whined Chooch, wiggling in his seat.

"You should've thought of that before," grumbled Luno. "Now will the two of you please be *quiet*?"

Luno ground the pod into gear. As he lifted off, he ignored the queasy feeling in the pit of his stomach

and concentrated on not crashing the delivery pod his first time out.

Luno uneasily wobbled off into the cosmos on his first delivery as his parents got smaller and smaller in the rearview screen.

CHAPTER FOUR

What to Do in the Event of a Death Spiral

Industro12 was now just a tiny dot and Luno was successfully piloting the delivery pod, when something whizzed past the windshield.

VROOOOOM!

Suddenly, everything in the cabin was spinning out of control! Luno found himself tumbling around with pizza boxes, candy bar wrappers, and tools.

"Aaahhh!" Chooch shrieked. "In the event of cabin decompression, an oxygen mask will automatically appear in front of you. Pull the mask toward you and—"

"What was *that*?!" Luno shouted over Chooch and the pod's emergency siren. "A *meteor*?"

"Quite possibly, Mr. Zorgoochi," Clive said, calmly

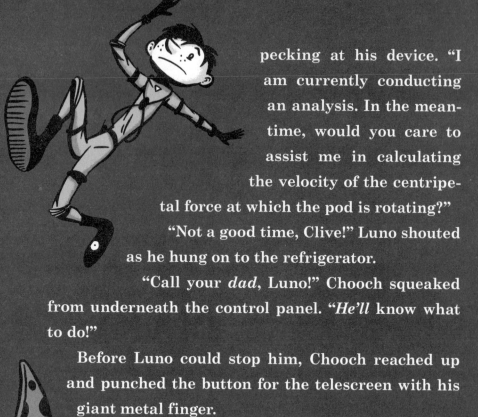

pecking at his device. "I am currently conducting an analysis. In the meantime, would you care to assist me in calculating the velocity of the centripetal force at which the pod is rotating?"

"Not a good time, Clive!" Luno shouted as he hung on to the refrigerator.

"Call your *dad*, Luno!" Chooch squeaked from underneath the control panel. "*He'll* know what to do!"

Before Luno could stop him, Chooch reached up and punched the button for the telescreen with his giant metal finger.

"Hey, buddy." Geo's face appeared. "How's it goin'?"

Luno pushed his face up as close as possible to the screen in order to block out the swirling debris.

"Oh, fine." Luno tried to sound casual, which was difficult with a 32-galactic-ton robot hugging his legs, muttering *we'regonnadiewe're gonnadiewe'regonnadie*.

"I forgot to give you a sweater, honey." Connie's face popped into view as Luno jammed a can of

scungilli into Chooch's
mouth to shut him up.

"I'm going to a *fire
planet*, Mom," Luno replied. "I
don't think I'll be chilly. Um, I just
called to say everything's fine. Gotta go. Bye!"

As Luno ended the transmission, he knew deep
down he'd like for his father to help him, but even with
thoughts of imminent danger flying around his head
and junk flying around the pod, he knew he *couldn't*.
He waited a long time to get out of the pizzeria and off
Industro12. He'd have to figure it out for himself.

Even though Clive may have been a genius and
Chooch may have had some of the same parts as the
pod, neither of them knew how to fly it. It was up to
Luno to regain control before he crashed into an asteroid. Or threw up.

As he crawled across the walls, it occurred
to him that the last time he felt this dizzy and
nauseous was when Roog accidentally knocked
him into the clothes dryer.

Clinging to anything that
wasn't spinning, Luno
managed to climb
back into the
driver's seat.

He strapped himself in and frantically pressed buttons, but nothing worked! *Ack!*

Luno searched his brain, but what to do in the event of a death spiral was definitely *not* covered in driver's ed.

Then he remembered what his father said. Luno gripped the steering stick and closed his eyes.

"You already know what to do," Luno whispered. "Now *do* it."

Without opening his eyes, Luno reached out and pressed the horizontal stabilizer button. Within moments, the pod was steadily humming to Inferno9 as if nothing had happened.

"Quantum Pizza nearly destroyed us, Mr. Zorgoochi," Clive announced calmly.

"Huh?" Luno opened his eyes and blinked.

"It was not a meteor, but a Quantum Pizza delivery ship that crossed our trajectory and nearly destroyed us," Clive said matter-of-factly, pecking away.

"Did somebody say *pizza*?" Chooch's head popped out from under the control panel where he was hiding. "Because I'm kinda hungry."

KA-CHUNK! KA-CHUNK! KA-*CHUNCK!*

Clive informed Luno that the sound they were hearing was a malfunctioning fan belt, which had been damaged in the tailspin. As an afterthought, Clive added that without a fully operational fan belt cooling the atomic engine, the pod would explode in about twenty minutes.

With no spare parts and a solid C average in Astral Mechanics, Luno tried not to panic and think of something to do.

"MOZZARELLA!" Luno suddenly shouted.

Even Chooch couldn't believe Luno was thinking of dairy products at a time like this, but Luno was too busy scraping the extra cheese off one of the pizzas in the oven in Chooch's chest to explain.

Before Clive could ask what his plan was, Luno already had his helmet on and was scurrying around the outside of the delivery pod. Luno was so excited about coming up with a brilliant solution to fix the fan belt, he forgot to be scared. With all his might, he pried open the engine panel. As he patched up the busted fan belt using the sticky mozzarella, Luno thought how proud his great-great-great-aunt Genia, who won awards for isolating the pizza molecule, would be of him right now, that is, if she were still alive.

"*That* ought to hold it," Luno said, back inside and unscrewing his helmet. Clive gave a nod of approval at Luno's quick thinking and Chooch cried tears of joy.

After mopping up Chooch's tears of joy, Luno slid into the pilot's seat and scanned the control panel.

Engine's atomic core temperature. *Check.*

Pizza temperature. *Check.*

Fan belt. *Um, check,* I hope.

Then a smile grew on Luno's lips.

Pilot's ability to handle a crisis. *Check!*

CHAPTER FIVE

A Hot Time on Inferno9

A flaming orange planet glowed angrily in the distance. Inferno9.

As Luno landed, he could already feel the high temperature rising up from the planet's smoldering surface right through the floor of the pod and through the soles of his space boots.

The three friends peered warily out the porthole. The landscape was a charred wasteland riddled with crevices spewing flames. It reminded Luno of his first attempt at making pizza.

He slipped on a pair of heat-resistant boots, a pair of gloves, and a space suit, then opened the oven in

Chooch's chest and slipped the super spicy-pizza with extra hot peppers into a thermal pizza pouch.

"Excuse me, Mr. Zorgoochi," said Clive, "but the surface temperature of Inferno9 is over 600 degrees. I hardly think you will need a thermal pouch to keep the pizza warm."

"I know," Luno replied. "I'm putting it in here to keep it from bursting into flames when it hits the atmosphere."

Clive nodded.

"All ready, Luno!" said Chooch, holding a stick with a marshmallow at the end of it. "Let's *go!*"

But Luno gently explained that he had to go alone.

"It could be *dangerous* out there, Chooch!" Luno said, as the giant robot rolled around on the floor kicking his feet and bawling.

"Well then, Mr. Zorgoochi," said Clive, "if it could be dangerous, why are *you* going?"

Luno knew it was pointless to try to explain to a super-intelligent, yet entirely clueless mutant bulb of garlic and a giant crybaby robot that he *had* to go. Alone. He needed to prove to his dad he could do this.

"*Because,*" said Luno as he climbed the ladder to the hatch.

"That is an entirely unsound, extremely unfounded, and highly unscientific reason," Clive said flatly.

It may have been unsound, unfounded, and unscientific, but Luno opened the hatch and climbed out anyway.

Waves of heat rippled up from the scorched ground and jets of fire shot out from sinkholes every few feet, keeping Luno on his toes. Luckily, he was used to the scorching heat, thanks to Roog forcing him to walk over hot coals in the kitchen's massive coal-fired oven every morning for the last few years. Luno never understood what it had to do with making pizza until now.

His space suit contracted from the heat and clung to his body, making his shorts ride up. Sweat poured from every pore, his eyes teared, and his hair felt like it

was on fire. The only time Luno was hotter than this was when he and his parents visited William10, the Zorgoochi's old retired delivery robot, at Rusty Acres on Planet Rur, where apparently elderly robots liked the weather hot and to eat dinner in the afternoon. In fact, it was so hot, the freckles on Luno's face actually slid down a quarter inch.

Hssssssss!

Luno spun around. It was a giant fire lizard!

It stood on a high ridge, switching its tail and spewing flames. Luno was frozen with fear as the lizard's yellow eyes scanned the fiery horizon and landed on him. It gave a hungry growl and began lumbering down

the ridge, flicking its tongue. Luno's brain finally de-frosted enough for him to get his feet moving. He didn't care in which direction, just as long as it was as far away as possible from the giant, hungry, fire-breathing lizard that would most definitely eat him, but not be-fore *cooking* him first.

To make matters worse, Luno saw a delivery ship in the distance and knew Quantum had already inter-cepted his order. But before he could reach the ship, it blasted off, leaving him in a cloud of red dust, which fortunately scared away the lizard, for the moment anyway.

After spitting out a few mouthfuls of soot, Luno heard the faint sound of laughter over a hill a few yards away. With pizza box firmly in hand, he climbed to the top and saw a group of Infernals, the giant fire crea-tures who live on Inferno9, finishing up a Quantum pizza.

Luno steeled himself and marched down the hill to-ward them.

"Pizza delivery!" Luno shouted, trying to sound confident and businesslike, but came off as somewhat terrified of being burnt to a crisp.

"Who are *you*?" the biggest Infernal asked, belching out a burst of flames.

"Zorgoochi Intergalactic Pizza," Luno croaked,

then cleared his throat. "Did you order a super-spicy pizza with extra hot peppers?"

"Yeah," the other one said. "We *did* and we just ate it, so *beat* it!"

Luno tried his best to explain without sounding scared utterly witless that Quantum intercepted the order and that *he* was actually delivering the pizza they ordered from Zorgoochi Intergalactic Pizza. Then Luno pulled the pizza out of the thermal pouch and it instantly burst into flames.

The Infernals looked at the fiery pizza and then at each other. The big one skeptically took a slice.

"Be careful not to burn the roof of your mouth!" Luno warned.

"Are you *kidding*?" the big one smiled. "We *love* when that happens!"

The Infernal took a bite and his eyes lit up, and then he devoured the whole slice.

"This is *way* better than that Quantum stuff," the big one said as he shoved another slice into his blazing mouth.

Hearing this, the other Infernals greedily grabbed slices of their own and gobbled them down as well. They ate and ate until there was nothing left but a burning pepper on the bottom of the fireproof box, which the fat one snatched up and tossed into his mouth.

Braaap! They all belched in unison, sending jets of fire into the air.

"That'll be 50,000 bux," Luno said, but then added meekly, "plus tip."

The Infernals looked at one another, then burst out laughing. The big one doubled over and pounded the ground with his flaming fist.

"W-what's so funny?" Luno asked.

"We ain't payin' you *squat*, squirt!" the other one said.

Luno just *knew* he couldn't go back to his father without the money for the delivery. He couldn't bear to see the disappointment on Dad's face like the time Luno had the brilliant idea of in addition to pizza *toppings*, why not have *bottomings*, too? What a mess *that* was.

Luno squared his shoulders and announced, "Well, you *have* to! You already ate the pizza and according to Galactic Pizza Convention Protocol number 432, 'the recipients must pay for any pizza they've eaten, absorbed through membranes, or disintegrated as a means of consumption,' which *means* . . ."

Luno shouted louder over the Infernals' laughter.

"WHICH *MEANS*—" Luno yelled.

"Which *means*," the big one said, as the flame on the tip of his nose nearly singed Luno's, "we ain't payin' you, so *scram!*"

Luno held the thermal pouch in front of him as the

Infernals blew flames right at him. As they paused to inhale, Luno slipped the pouch over himself and ran. It was difficult enough navigating his way back to the ship inside the pouch, but the Infernals were shooting flames at his butt, which made it that much more difficult to run.

Unzipping the pouch a bit and peeking out, Luno caught sight of the delivery pod.

"Start up the pod!" Luno shouted. "Fire up the engine!"

The hatch popped open and Chooch's head popped out.

"I don't know *how*!" Chooch shouted, and then he disappeared.

"Is there a manual available so I may learn how to start the engine, Mr. Zorgoochi?" Clive's head suddenly

appeared. "A schematic diagram of the delivery pod would also be helpful."

"Just press the ignition button!" Luno shouted.

Looking back, Luno noticed that the Infernals had given up the chase, but then he stopped in his tracks. Luno had bigger problems ahead of him. The fire lizard was back and blocking his way to the pod.

Hsssss! It hungrily paced back and forth, determined not to let its dinner get away a second time.

As Luno locked eyes with it, he carefully bent at the knees and picked up a flaming rock and drew his arm back. As he flung it with all his might, Chooch's head reappeared and asked, "*Which* button do I press?"

Tonk!

The sound the rock made when it hit Chooch's head sounded like two coconuts knocking together, which was enough to distract the lizard so Luno could make a mad dash around the other side of the pod.

"Ouch," Chooch said, rubbing his head.

Luno dove into the hatch and slammed it shut.

He dropped into the pilot's seat, jammed the ignition button, and slammed the pod into gear.

Hsssss! The lizard, now angrier than ever, breathed flames directly at the windshield.

As they lifted off, the lizard whipped its tail and hissed some more, but in a few moments, it was nothing but a dark green speck on an angry blazing planet. And after a while, Inferno9 was just another dot in a deep black expanse, no different from the hundreds of others Luno saw around him.

"Whew!" Luno breathed as he set the coordinates for his next delivery. "I can't believe we got out of there without getting hurt!"

"Um, *Luno*?" said Chooch, pointing at Luno's boots.

He looked down. His boots were not only

smoldering, but the soles were completely burned away and his bare feet were showing! A curl of smoke floated up Luno's nostril, reminding him of the last time he smelled this familiar aroma, when he made a calzone so spicy, his dad had to put it out with a fire extinguisher.

"What an *idiot* I am." Luno sighed, pulling off his charred boots and putting a new pair on. "I didn't even get paid for my very first delivery!"

"It's okay, Luno," said Chooch. "As long as you're safe and browned."

"No, Chooch, it's *not* okay!" Luno snapped. "My dad's going to *kill* me!"

"I must agree with you, Mr. Zorgoochi," said Clive. "This is unacceptable. I suggest you return to Inferno9

and inform the Infernals of Galactic Pizza Convention Protocol number 432, 'the recipient must pay for any pizza—'"

"Don't you think I *did* that already?" Luno groaned, his head in his hands.

"Well, *we* still love you!" cried Chooch as he lunged toward Luno and Clive with open giant metal arms. "Group hug!"

"Okay! *Okay!*" Luno gasped, locked in a death embrace, smashed against Clive. "Thank you, now let me *go!*"

"Define 'love,' Mr. Zorgoochi," said Clive.

CHAPTER SIX

Fuzzy Wuzzies Aren't So Fuzzy

KA-CHUNK! KA-CHUNK! KA-*CHUNCK*!

"What's *that*?" Chooch asked.

"I believe it is the sound of the delivery pod's auxiliary fan belt coming loose again, which will soon stop cooling the engine and cause the atomic reactor to overheat, then explode," Clive said, not looking up from his device. "So you may consider locating a replacement part."

Luno quickly switched on the radar to find a repair shop in the vicinity, but then realized he'd have to use his dad's cosmic credit account to pay for it. Luno could just hear Dad scolding him for wasting money when he could've just fixed the fan belt himself. Luno would have to figure out another way, a way that would show Dad he could deal with something as simple as a busted fan belt and not blow up the pod (or himself). However, it was kind of difficult to come up with a solution with the echo of Chooch's metal stomach constantly growling and Clive's litany of annoying questions about absolutely everything around them.

"Hey, *look!*" Chooch suddenly shouted, pointing out the windshield.

Luno turned to see a massive holo billboard hovering over a lone asteroid in the distance.

"'Free Spare Parts'!" Luno read, squinting at the fuzzy letters. "Let's *go!*"

"I am afraid that is not what is written on the sign, Mr. Zorgoochi," said Clive. "It actually reads 'Mold Spore Convention' and I strongly suggest we attend."

"No it *doesn't!*" Chooch shouted. "It says 'Fresh Baked Cookies' and I'm *starving!*"

They may have argued about what the sign actually said, but all agreed that they should land on that asteroid *immediately*.

Luno didn't have much time to think about how odd it was that each of them read something different, as they were touching down and scrambling to be the first one out of the pod.

"Hello?" Luno called as he swung open the hatch and climbed down to the dusty surface.

Through the greenish haze, Luno spotted a towering structure nearby, which he headed toward with Clive and Chooch trailing behind.

"So where are all the *cookies*, Luno?" asked Chooch, looking around.

"We must locate the *convention center,* Mr. Zorgoochi," said Clive. "We do not want to miss the mold spores."

It didn't take Luno very long to figure out that there *were* no free spare parts, let alone a mold spore convention *or* cookies. The place had an air of desolation and emptiness. Luno moved forward with a feeling of dread in the pit of his stomach, but knew he had to fix the pod, even if it meant facing mortal danger. Or worse, a disappointed dad.

The closer they came to the strange jury-rigged mess of metal beams, engine parts, and various space junk, the more Luno's head throbbed. Hovering above was the massive buzzing holo billboard.

"What *is* this thing?" asked Chooch, touching a metal girder.

"I think it's a transmitter that beams out the signal for the sign," Luno said, looking up at the 100-story-tall words "Free Spare Parts" flickering high above them. At least that's what *Luno* saw. He rubbed his eyes. His head pounded along with the strange whirring pulse the structure seemed to give off.

"Actually, this somewhat ramshackle assemblage is not only a transmitter," said Clive, "but a *receiver* as well."

In the far-off distance, Luno spotted what appeared to be a small ship and three dark silhouettes. He waved at them through the mist, but they didn't wave back. Strange.

As they cautiously walked toward the figures, Luno thought that maybe they could help him find a replacement fan belt.

Of course there was always the distinct possibility that they would kill him.

"I'm *scared*, Luno," said Chooch, hanging on to Luno's arm, dragging him down. "I changed my mind. I don't want cookies anymore. Let's *go!*"

"Pardon me," Clive said, approaching one of the figures. "Can you direct us to the mold spore convention?"

Luno walked up and saw that Clive was talking to an empty space suit.

"I say," said Clive, "which way to the convention?"

"It's just a *suit*, Clive," said Luno. "There's no one in it."

The ship, like the space suits, appeared to have been abandoned for junk a long time ago. Luno walked around to the ship's engine panel. It opened with a long *squeeeak*.

"Hey! Just what we needed!" said Luno, yanking out a fan belt and examining it. "I guess there *were* spare parts after all. What a break!"

As Luno happily hurried back to the delivery pod to replace the part, Clive and Chooch followed him.

"We are going to miss the *convention*, Mr. Zorgoochi," said Clive.

"Don't you *get* it?" said Luno. "There *is* no convention!"

Luno climbed to the top of the delivery pod. The ship and the space suits were probably dumped there years ago. The galaxy was full of space trash. And the billboard, well, it was probably just malfunctioning and no one had bothered to fix it. Besides, none of this mattered because he had found a fan belt, so now he could repair the pod and make his next delivery.

But most importantly, his father would be proud of him.

Luno yanked on the pod's engine panel and thought again about how weird it was that each of them saw something *different* on the sign, something each of them *wanted*, almost as if the holo billboard could somehow project their thoughts. But before he came to the conclusion that it was kind of eerie, the panel popped open with a p-*twang*!

"This'll just take a few minutes," Luno's voice echoed from inside the engine.

Starved for intellectual stimulation, Clive scanned the asteroid's surface with his device to determine its molecular composition. Starved for cookies, Chooch wandered around looking for some, wondering why anyone would be so mean as to advertise fresh baked cookies when there really weren't any.

Chooch meandered aimlessly until a small noise caught his attention. It was a bit like a squeak combined with a giggle. He looked around, and out from the craggy ground right below his feet popped a fuzzy little critter.

Squeak! Giggle giggle. *Squeak!*

It was the cutest thing Chooch had ever seen! The little fuzzy creature looked up at him with saucer eyes and cheerfully squeaked some more. Charmed, Chooch bent down and gently offered his giant metal hand. After giving it a few sniffs, the critter trustingly climbed into his palm.

Chooch held the little fuzz ball and it affectionately rubbed against his cheek, making a sort of purring sound. This got Chooch so excited, he almost started clapping his hands in delight, but remembered he was holding the critter and that would not have been a very good idea. He called Clive over to see his new little friend.

By the time Clive arrived, there were several darling fuzz balls climbing all over Chooch, gently pawing him with their tiny raccoon-like hands and purring loudly, which seemed to summon even more of them from underground.

"Look at all the Fuzzy Wuzzies, Clive!" Chooch said. "That's the name I just made up for these little guys!"

"Hmmm," said Clive as he scanned the creatures with his device. "Carbon-based life-form, mammal, most likely sentient, quite possibly intelligent."

"And they're *cute*!" Chooch said, giggling as they nuzzled his face.

"Define 'cute,'" said Clive as a critter climbed up his leg.

"All set!" Luno said, striding up to Clive and Chooch, now both crawling with the darling downy soft creatures. "What are *those*?"

"I believe Chooch has named them Fuzzy Wuzzies," said Clive. "But I have decided to categorize them as *Bellus creaturus*. I will present a full report of my findings in twenty-four hours, Mr. Zorgoochi."

Chooch asked, then *begged* Luno to let him bring a few of them home. He promised he would feed and walk them and Luno wouldn't have to do a *thing*. Really!

Luno couldn't deny they were cute and began to

actually consider taking a few home as a critter rubbed against his neck and purred.

"They look hungry!" said Chooch. "What do you think they eat?"

"According to my readings," said Clive, brushing a critter off his device, "these creatures are the only living organic matter on this entire asteroid, which means there is no sustenance for them here."

Luno thought this was rather odd as one of them crawled up his leg, which wouldn't have been so bad, but it was from the *inside* of his space suit!

As Luno shook his leg to get it out, more critters climbed on the three of them and giggled and squeaked, which seemed to cause even *more* of them to pour out from the ground. Soon Luno, Chooch, and even Clive were wriggling around giggling, looking like they were wearing living fur coats.

Luno rolled around on the ground to get them off, but then found himself rolling down a hill into a massive crater. He got up, still crawling with them, and saw something very strange.

"Hey, you guys!" Luno shouted. "Look at all these ships—*ouch!*"

One of the critters *nipped* him. Covered in creatures, Clive and Chooch lumbered down the hill and saw a vast expanse of abandoned spaceships, some partially disassembled. Luno wondered what they were all doing there. Soon more critters were nipping at him, some actually *biting*! Ouch!

"Naughty, naughty Fuzzy Wuzzy!" said Chooch, yanking one off his finger. "Ow!"

"Yes," agreed Clive. "Please refrain from biting me. It causes me to experience what I understand to be a sensation called pain."

"Yee-*ouch*!" Luno cried. Several critters bit down hard and it really *hurt*! "Let's get out of here!"

As the three of them ran to the pod covered in cute, but increasingly vicious creatures, Luno tripped. He got up and saw what he tripped over: a shredded space suit!

"Help!" Chooch cried. Luno turned to see that he tripped, too, but not over a space suit. *It was an alien skeleton!*

And it was stripped to the bone.

Luno quickly helped Chooch to his feet and they desperately hurried toward the ship. A steady stream of the adorable little creatures poured out of the ground and were in hot pursuit!

"I have formulated a theory on how the *Bellus creaturus*, or the more colloquially known Fuzzy Wuzzies, acquire nourishment, Mr. Zorgoochi," said Clive. "Since there is no actual sustenance on this asteroid, they must attract food *to* it."

"Wait a minute—*ouch!*" said Luno, pulling them off his head. "You mean *we're* their *food*? How?"

"The reason we each perceived something different on the billboard was due to the fact that the structure is both a transmitter *and* receiver," Clive calmly explained. "These creatures cleverly constructed a device that received our deepest desires through our brain waves and then transmitted them back to each of us through the sign in order to attract us to this asteroid."

"So these cute-looking little things actually made that transmitter/receiver harvested from the ships back there?" Luno asked, climbing the delivery pod's ladder.

"I assume by 'cute,'" said Clive, peeling a few critters off his glasses, "you mean cunning and bloodthirsty."

Chooch asked what happened to the pilots of all of those ships, but before Clive could deliver his homicidal hypothesis, Luno cut him off and told them they were all off finding a snack for the Fuzzy Wuzzies.

Luno shook off as many as he could as he climbed up the pod's ladder, opened the hatch, and jumped in. In a moment his head popped up and he tossed out a few frozen pizzas from the onboard freezer.

Immediately, the critters swarmed off Clive and Chooch and all over the pizzas. They quickly climbed into the pod and Luno slammed the hatch, but had to open it again to toss out one last critter.

Squeak! Giggle giggle. *Squeak!*

As he fired up the engine, Luno saw that the evil Fuzzy Wuzzies had already consumed the pizzas (and the box) and were turning their hungry attention toward the pod. As they swarmed all over it, the sound of thousands of tiny nibbling teeth echoed as Luno ground the pod into gear and turned on the windshield wiper to brush a few of them off.

"I don't want to call them Fuzzy Wuzzies anymore," said Chooch, rubbing his arms and legs. "From now on I'm calling them Bitey Whities."

No sooner did the pod lift off and the last Fuzzy Wuzzy drop off, laser fire was pinging off the sides of the delivery pod!

P-twang! P-*twing*!

Luno looked in the rearview screen.

"Quantum delivery ships at six o'clock!" Luno shouted, dodging their fire.

"I believe you are incorrect, Mr. Zorgoochi," Clive said.

"Yeah!" said Chooch, pointing at the control panel clock. "It's only *three o'clock!*"

Using every bit of his driving skills, Luno evaded Quantum's fire; spinning, turning, loop-the-looping, zigzagging. He'd never driven like this before, but somehow at this very moment he just *knew how.* It was a lot like playing his favorite electro game, Asteroid Dodger, except he couldn't pause it to go to the bathroom and if he blew himself up, he couldn't just start over again. He'd be *dead.*

"Quantum Pizza is quite ruthless," said Clive.

"Yeah," shouted Chooch from underneath the control panel. "They don't have *Ruth*! Whoever *she* is."

Luno knew Clive was right. Quantum wasn't going to give up, but what could he do?

He had no weapons.

No ideas.

And no choice.

Luno did the only thing he could think of: hide in the asteroid belt dead ahead. Maybe the Quantum ships would be satisfied they ran him off the main spaceway and go back to their deliveries.

Luno gritted his teeth, slammed his foot down on the accelerator, and aimed the pod toward the relative safety of the dangerous mass of deadly sharp-pointed floating asteroids.

Then he looked in the rearview.

They were still chasing him.

It was hard enough driving at top speed dodging massive rocks and laser fire, but it was that much harder with Chooch blubbering buckets of tears and muttering, "There are several emergency exits on this aircraft. Please take a few moments now to locate your nearest exit . . ."

Drawing on the many hours he had clocked playing Asteroid Dodger, Luno zipped through the maze of planetoids and, much to his surprise, didn't kill himself. If his mother could see him now, she'd never complain about him playing electro games ever again!

After gaining a considerable lead, Luno managed to hide the pod in the center of a cluster of asteroids and land on one. The Quantum ships passed overhead a few moments later, buzzing around like angry space hornets looking for him.

As they sat parked on one of the asteroids among

the giant rocks, Luno held his breath and he held his hand over Chooch's mouth to keep him quiet. Clive, on the other hand, was entirely unaware of the life and death situation they were in and calmly pecked away at his device.

It felt like an eternity, but the Quantum ships eventually gave up and returned to the main spaceway.

Whew.

CHAPTER SEVEN

Hold the Mushrooms

"I changed my mind, Luno," Chooch whined. "I wanna go home—*now!*"

Luno patiently explained they had just two more deliveries to go and then they would be heading back to the pizzeria. He was determined to make up for not getting paid by the Infernals by being the best delivery boy *ever* and getting two great big tips. Then he'd give them to his dad as payment for the pizza he got stiffed on.

Geo would never have to know.

"Planet Fungi," Luno said, pointing to a tiny tan-colored dot on the dashboard radar screen. "Our next delivery."

Within moments, Luno was making a perfect three-point landing. The only problem was, the pod had four wheels. He still had to work on that.

"Stay put," Luno told Clive and Chooch as he slid the large pizza with extra mushrooms out of Chooch's oven and into a box. "I'll be right back."

Right on cue, Chooch threw another temper tantrum. Luno first tried to reason with him. When *that* didn't work, he tried being firm, but couldn't be heard over Chooch's crying.

"Oh, all *right*," Luno sighed. "You can come."

Chooch immediately stopped crying as if flipping a switch. In fact Chooch actually *did*. It was a small red one on his lower left side.

"I would like to accompany you as well in order to gather information about this Planet Fungi," said Clive, following them out of the hatch.

Luno just shook his head. What was the point of arguing? That would only make him later than he already was.

Luno climbed down the side of the pod and planted a foot into the moist ground. Planet Fungi was dark, damp, and kind of creepy.

They made their way through a forest of giant pale trees, but upon closer inspection, Luno discovered they weren't trees at all. They were enormous *mushrooms*!

"Why would someone who lived on a planet with all these mushrooms want a *mushroom pizza*?" Luno asked. "It doesn't make any sense."

As they trudged on, Luno picked his head up, threw back his shoulders, and smiled, determined to be the most cheerful and courteous delivery boy in the Mezzaluna Galaxy. He was sure he was going to get that great big tip!

And then it hit him.

What if Quantum already got here first? What if . . .

Luno stopped himself, shook it off, and forced himself to hold the pizza box high and proud. His father, mother, Zorgoochi Intergalactic Pizza, and pretty much

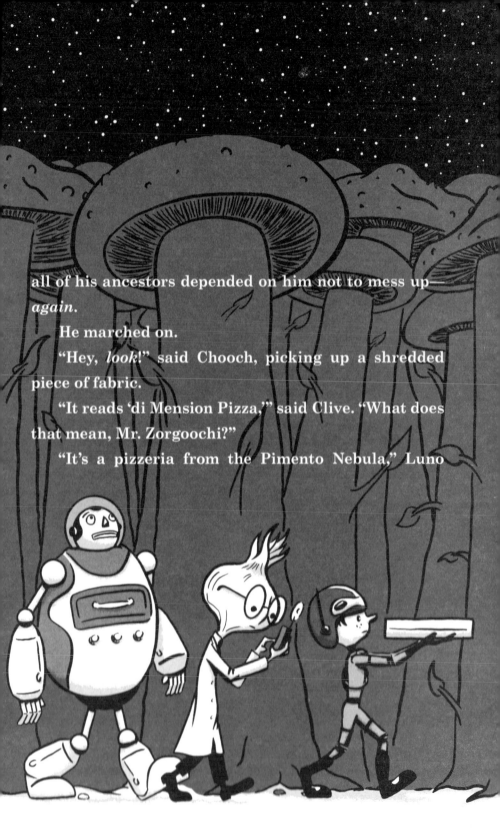

all of his ancestors depended on him not to mess up—
again.

He marched on.

"Hey, *look*!" said Chooch, picking up a shredded piece of fabric.

"It reads 'di Mension Pizza.'" said Clive. "What does that mean, Mr. Zorgoochi?"

"It's a pizzeria from the Pimento Nebula," Luno

said, examining what looked to be part of a delivery boy's cap. "*That*'s weird."

Luno had heard of di Mension Pizza. It was another family-owned pizzeria, just like Zorgoochi.

Then Luno noticed something else—a torn piece of what appeared to be a pizza box. He held it up close and examined the microscopic circuitry running through the cardboard. He'd heard about a new kind of delivery box that had moisture control built right in so the pizza didn't get soggy, but couldn't remember which pizzeria had invented it.

"Uncle Cosmo's Pizza," read Chooch, holding up another shredded piece of fabric.

"Hey! *That*'s the place that invented this box," said Luno, tossing it away. "I wonder what all this stuff is doing here."

Before Clive could submit his theory, the ground began to rumble, shaking them so much they lost their balance and fell to the ground.

When Luno looked up and saw the giant mushrooms uprooting themselves, he knew he had to get out of there—*fast!*

Luno was helping Clive and Chooch to their feet when a massive white stalk wrapped around him and lifted him up to the very cap of the mushroom. Luno found himself dangling before what looked like a face.

"I am *Champignon!*" bellowed the mushroom.

"*Queen* of Planet Fungi! Genuflect before me, tiny human!"

"Huh?" asked Luno.

"*Bow!*" shouted the queen. Her breath smelled like delicious fresh mushrooms and wet dirt.

Luno tried as best he could, but it wasn't easy. He straightened up and spoke in a confident yet polite manner, hoping this was merely the way pizza delivery boys were greeted on Planet Fungi.

"Did you order a large Zorgoochi Pizza with extra mushrooms, ma'am?" Luno asked, holding the box up high, but then he turned to see several mushrooms emerging from the darkness waddling toward him.

"Legatus!" shouted the queen, clapping two of her stalks together. "Extract the receptacle from the human!"

"Huh?" the mushroom asked.

"Take the *box!*" the queen said, smacking the mushroom in the back of the cap.

"Yes, Your queen-atude!" said Legatus, who snatched the box from Luno and presented it to Queen Champignon. Then she opened it.

A loud *gasp* echoed throughout the forest. When the queen saw the pizza with extra mushrooms, her head drooped down and she wept. Then she looked up to the sky and bellowed, "Oh, sorrow! Oh, despair! I will avenge your demise, my fallen porcini subjects!"

The group of giant mushrooms stared woefully at the sliced mushrooms on the pizza, then put their stalks around one another and whimpered. The queen wailed and shouted about the tragedy of innocent little fungi being viciously and needlessly slaughtered.

"What's *fungi*?" asked Chooch, who was now being lifted up by another of the queen's stalks next to a dangling Luno.

"Unicellular, multicellular, or syncytial spore-producing organisms, including molds, yeast, and mushrooms," said Clive, still on the ground, pecking away at his device, hardly noticing their dire predicament.

"Oh, *now* I get it!" Chooch smiled. "This is a *mushroom* planet! Hey, Luno! Did you know—"

"*Silence!*" shouted the queen.

Then the queen turned to Luno.

"Do you know what we do on Planet Fungi to rogue assassins of defenseless mushrooms who murder them and place them on pizzas?" asked the queen.

"You pay them and give them a great big tip?" Luno asked hopefully.

Gales of grim laughter erupted among the mushrooms until Queen Champignon raised a stalk, quickly silencing them.

The queen drew Luno closer and, with an evil grin, said, "Quid pro quo."

"Huh?" Luno asked.

"What do *squids* have to do with it?" asked Chooch.

"Not *squid*! *Quid*!" shouted the frustrated queen. "*Quid* pro quo! We place *them* on a pizza!"

Luno gulped. Now he was *positive* he wasn't getting a tip. And he wasn't so sure if he was getting out of there *alive* either.

The mushrooms rubbed their horrible stalks together in anticipation of the deadly pizza party to come. The queen clapped her leaves and the group of mushrooms parted, revealing a full kitchen right there in the middle of the forest complete with a colossal wood-burning oven!

"Hey, *look*!" Legatus said, pointing at Clive. "Garlic!"

"We'll only use half," Queen Champignon said, picking him up. "Garlic gives me indigestion."

Holding Luno, Clive, and Chooch, the queen shuffled over to the makeshift kitchen. She explained with wicked delight that she'd been ordering mushroom pizzas to lure delivery boys and then eating them as fitting revenge!

"Then aren't *you* committing a similar atrocity?" asked Clive.

"*Silence*, garlic!" Queen Champignon bellowed. "I haven't even ingested you yet and you're already giving me indigestion!"

Luno, Clive, and Chooch helplessly hung there as the queen ordered the other mushrooms around.

"Can we go home *now*, Luno?" whined Chooch.

"I agree with Chooch, Mr. Zorgoochi," said Clive. "I believe I have gathered enough data about Planet Fungi and I am also ready to leave."

As Luno desperately tried to figure a way out, he watched one of the mushrooms spin a massive glob of dough in the air, much better than him, he noticed. Then the mushroom laid the dough out on a monolithic pizza stone and began to create the crust.

With an evil grin, the queen raised Luno, Clive, and Chooch into the air as the rest of the mushrooms gathered around and cheered.

"Now to exact retribution for our fallen comrades!" Queen Champignon announced to her mushroom minions.

"Huh?" the mushrooms asked.

The queen sighed and rubbed her weary eyes.

"I'm going to put them on the pizza," she said flatly.

The mushrooms cheered!

Luno looked helplessly at Clive and Chooch as the queen carried them over to the pizza waiting for them on the massive stone.

"We're up a creek without a poodle!" whined Chooch. "What are we gonna *do*?"

"Now don't forget to spit out the bones!" the queen reminded her minions.

When he heard this, Chooch started to wail uncontrollably. "We're gonna *die!*"

"Bravery" wasn't in Chooch's vocabulary, nor were lots of other words.

"Don't cry, Chooch!" Luno said, even though he wanted to join him.

Chooch couldn't stop and soon his tears were pouring over Queen Champignon.

"I order you to stop that incessant blubbering!" the queen cried.

Chooch's tears continued to flow all over the queen as well as all of the mushrooms, and right before Luno's very eyes, the mushrooms started to somehow get *bigger!* What was happening?

"I *command* you!" gurgled the queen. "Cease!"

Then Luno remembered a kitchen tip from Roog: Mushrooms should only be cleaned with a vegetable brush or damp cloth, but *never* underwater because they're *extremely absorbent!*

The queen tried to shake Chooch off her stalk, but Luno told him to hang on; and soon all of the mushrooms were so bloated and squishy, they couldn't move!

As Luno, Clive, and Chooch now easily slipped out of the stalks, the queen burbled, "Seize them!" but none of them could understand her and even if they did, they couldn't really do anything about it.

Luno dashed to the delivery pod as fast as he could and scrambled up the ladder, then opened the hatch. He dropped to the floor and sprang into the pilot's seat. As he furiously jabbed at the ignition button, he heard Clive climb into the pod and Chooch fall to the floor with a *crash*. With his crew present and accounted for, Luno slammed the pod into gear and floored the accelerator.

They bolted into the sky and soon Planet Fungi was just another dot in the rearview screen.

"Well," said Chooch, "all's swell that ends swell!"

Luno smiled. He had to agree, but then he realized he hadn't gotten paid for *this* delivery, either. There was no way he was ever going to get a big enough tip from his third delivery, to Planet Freezorg, whatever *that* was, to make up for not getting paid for two whole pizzas.

What was *Dad* going to say?

Just as he was feeling himself falling into a spiral of fear, anxiety, and depression, the entire pod was jolted with a *PANG*, bringing him back to reality.

"Quantum delivery ship at six o'clock!" shouted Chooch.

But when Luno looked in the rearview screen there was nothing. Then he looked up at the windshield. *It was dead ahead!*

As he dodged the Quantum ship's laser fire, Luno shouted, "What do you *mean six* o'clock? It's *twelve* o'clock!"

"No it *isn't*," said Chooch, crawling under the control panel.

"I am afraid Chooch is correct, Mr. Zorgoochi," Clive said, pointing at the dashboard clock. "It *is* six o'clock."

Rather than explain the concept of hour location, Luno concentrated on the far more pressing matter of their rival pizzeria once again trying to take them out.

"I must say, Mr. Zorgoochi," said Clive, calmly observing Luno perform one cunning move after the other, "the way Quantum delivery ships locate us is quite uncanny."

"Yeah." Chooch peeked out and agreed, "They don't use *cans*!"

Luno fell into an almost trancelike state as he found himself anticipating where the Quantum ship would fire next. This went way beyond playing Asteroid Dodger and Luno knew it. The other thing that dawned on him was, unlike the last time, there were no clusters of asteroids for him to hide in.

However, up ahead was a massive yawning vortex, blacker than the blackest space swirling in the distance, sucking up everything that came near it.

"Look!" gasped Luno. "A *wormhole*!"

"That is *impossible*, Mr. Zorgoochi," said Clive, not looking up from his device. "Wormholes are merely *theoretical*."

"Is it full of giant *space worms*?" Chooch gasped.

"The simplest explanation would be that a wormhole is a shortcut through spacetime to another dimension, time, or area in the universe," said Clive. "Imagine spacetime as a two-dimensional plane which is folded together, creating a bridge. Now, that bridge—"

"*Not* a good time for a physics lesson, Clive!" shouted Luno.

"As I said," added Clive, "wormholes are only hypothetical."

"Well, it looks pretty real to *me*!" said Luno as he continued to dodge Quantum's fire and avoid the wormhole's irresistible gravitational pull at the same time.

"We're gonna *die*!" whimpered Chooch from under the control panel.

"The logical action to take," said Clive, "would be to confront them directly, Mr. Zorgoochi."

Luno knew that Clive was probably right, but was afraid that *Chooch* was probably right, maybe even *more* so. If he only had the Golden Anchovy to protect him, but like his dad said, that was for fun. This was for *real*.

Luno didn't know what else to do. He stopped resisting the irresistible pull of the wormhole and just let go.

As the tiny Zorgoochi delivery pod was sucked into the vacuum, a feeling of shame washed over Luno.

He was running away.

Again.

The orange emergency lights in the cockpit flashed and the siren blared as Clive calmly tightened his seat belt and Chooch rocked back and forth under the control panel, muttering, "In the event of decompression, an oxygen mask will appear in front of you. To start the flow of oxygen, pull the mask towards you . . ."

"I'm sorry, Dad," Luno whispered.

Then everything went black.

CHAPTER EIGHT

Through the Wormhole

Luno pushed open the front door to Zorgoochi Intergalactic Pizza. The familiar aroma of tomato sauce filled his nose and the heat from the pizza ovens warmed his bones. He was finally home.

"Son!" Geo said with a twinkle in his eye, arms open wide. "I'm so *proud* of you!"

Luno smiled and slid his hand into his pocket.

Geo looked down at Luno's open palm and his arms fell to his sides.

"Where's the money from the deliveries, Luno?" Geo asked.

Luno looked down.

"I," Luno muttered, "I-I don't know."

"*Brutto Malo!*" Geo cursed. "We *need* that money, Luno!" His father's hands balled into tight angry fists as he moved closer. Luno backed up toward the door. He never saw his father so *mad* before. It scared him.

"Luno, you will *never* be good enough to take over this pizzeria!" Geo bellowed. "*Never!*"

Luno turned and ran out the door.

"How could you let us down, Luno?" Connie wept. He turned to see his mother standing in front of the pizzeria crying and futilely waving her hands at the sign, which now read Quantum Pizza.

Geo burst through the door and ran after Luno!

"You let us *all* down, Luno!" dozens of voices wailed. He turned to see Solaro, Vulcanelli, Tomino, and all the rest of his dead ancestors pouring out of the pizzeria chasing him, too!

Luno tried to run faster, but could barely move. He looked down. He was knee-deep in melted mozzarella.

Suddenly, his father's giant hand clamped down on his shoulder. It felt cold and hard like metal.

"Luno!" Geo shouted. "Luno!"

Luno tried to get away, but he couldn't.

"*Luno!*"

Luno opened his eyes. Chooch was standing over him, shaking his shoulder.

"Luno! Luno, wake *up*!" Chooch said. "Guess *what*? We're not dead! Isn't that *great*?"

Luno blinked and looked around. He was still in the delivery pod. There were pizza boxes, tools, and trash all over, but Chooch was right. They *weren't* dead.

They were at the other end of the wormhole.

"Hmmm," said Clive. "It appears that wormholes are *not* theoretical, but indeed *fact*, Mr. Zorgoochi. I will have a full report for you by tomorrow morning."

This was all well and good for Clive's research, but Luno had no idea where or *when* or even *which dimension* they were in. He sat down and scraped the pepperoni off the control panel, then pecked away at the instruments, trying to get a read on their time, space, or dimensional location, but he had no luck.

To continue their lack of good luck or perhaps abundance of bad, Luno heard a familiar sound.

Ka-*chunk*!

It was the fan belt again.

With smoke pouring from the engine panel, the pod managed to sputter and rattle to a nearby planetoid before it overheated and blew up.

Luno opened the hatch and stuck his head out. He couldn't quite place the aroma. Some sort of soft cheese on a desolate asteroid? Luno chalked it up to a cosmic cross-breeze or to his socks needing to be changed more often. No matter, he had a fan belt to fix *again* and there was no time for food. As he walked across the hood of the pod, Luno looked around. A desolate expanse with a mountain range in the distance.

He would have to figure out a way to patch up the fan belt without any spare parts or help. Luno sighed deeply, then knelt down and opened the engine panel. He ducked his head in and reached into the engine.

"Luno?"

Bang!

"What?" he snapped, rubbing the top of his head.

"I'm *bored*," said Chooch.

Luno shook his head and rolled his eyes, then ducked back into the engine.

"Mr. Zorgoochi?"

Bang!

"*What?*" Luno asked, rubbing his head again.

"Being that you still have one more delivery to execute," said Clive, "I recommend you repair the pod's auxiliary fan belt immediately."

Luno sighed, and then ducked back in.

"Hello!"

Bang!

"WHAT?" Luno shouted.

He pulled his head out and looked down, then gasped.

"Can I help?" a tall, wizened alien asked. He was

dressed in a long brown robe and flanked by several similarly dressed aliens of various shapes and sizes.

"How would *he* know if you could help him?" a short one said to the tall one.

"Hmmm, I guess you're right," the tall one said, scratching his chin, and then turned to Luno. "I guess I can't help you."

The tall alien turned to leave, but then turned back.

"Unless it has to do with engines," he said.

"Yes!" said Luno, relieved. "It *does*!"

"*Well!*" chirped the tall alien. "Then I *really* can't help you. I don't know a thing about engines."

Luno furrowed his brow and said, "Thanks a *lot*."

"You're welcome!" The tall alien smiled, turned, and started walking toward the mountain range with the other aliens trailing close behind in a line.

"Wait!" Luno called. He climbed down from the pod and caught up with them. "Where *am* I?"

The tall alien stopped, causing the rest of them to bump into one another. He gave Luno an incredulous look, and then turned to the others, who looked equally confused. He shrugged.

"You're right *there*," the tall alien said, pointing at Luno.

They started to walk away again, but Luno caught up with them and waved his arms around. "No! I mean *where am I?*"

"Well," the tall alien said, "you used to be over *there*, but now you're over *here*."

Luno realized he wasn't going to get anywhere and was *sure* they weren't going to help him fix the fan belt, so he gave up and walked back to the pod.

Clive and Chooch approached Luno.

"Can we go *now*, Luno?" Chooch whined.

"Have you completed the necessary repairs, Mr. Zorgoochi?" Clive asked.

Luno wearily shook his head.

"*Zorgoochi?*" the tall alien asked. "Now where have I heard that name before?"

"Why, *he* just said it," the short one replied, pointing at Clive.

"Ah, I guess you're right," said the tall alien, then turned to the others and said, "Come now, fellows. Time to practice Tai Cheese!"

Luno stood there watching the nine robed aliens make their way toward the foot of the mountain when a thought suddenly struck him. He tried to push it out of his mind, but just *couldn't*.

Luno called to the tall alien, "You wouldn't happen to be *Master Uno*, would you?"

The tall alien stopped, causing the others to bump into one another once more.

"I don't know," he replied, scratching his head. "I was yesterday."

Luno gasped. His body crawled with goose bumps. His heart pounded. He was almost too afraid to move.

"You *can't be*," Luno said.

"Then I'm probably not," said the tall alien.

"Unless you *are*," said the short one.

"I never thought of that," said the tall one.

Luno ran up and pointed to each alien. "That means you're Due, you're Tre, you're Quattro, you're Cinque, you're Sei, you're Sette, you're Otto, and you're Nove!"

"Now that *that's* been cleared up," said Master Uno, "let's get going, fellows."

Chooch asked, "So who *are* these guys, Luno?"

"They're the *Mozzarella Monks*!" Luno shouted.

"*Really?* I can't believe it!" cried Chooch, but then asked, "Um, who are *they*?"

Luno explained that his dad told him stories about the fabled Mozza-rella Monks, the greatest cheese mak-ers in the universe, who lived on the enchanted Planet of Formaggio. Only *they* held the secret of making

the finest cheese in the Mezzaluna Galaxy and, in the most rare instance, shared those secrets with someone they felt worthy.

"My father told me you taught my great-great-great-great-great-grandfather Solaro Zorgoochi how to make cheese," said Luno.

"Solaro Zorgoochi was our brightest student!" said Quattro.

"But this is not the case for *all* of our students," said Due, as the monks nodded in agreement.

"Hmmm, *Zorgoochi*," said Master Uno. "I *thought* you looked familiar. You've inherited Solaro's nose."

"Wow!" said Luno. "You can tell I have his super sense of smell just by *looking* at me?"

"Oh, *do* you?" Master Uno asked. "I just meant you have a big nose like his."

Upon hearing that Luno was a descendant of their most talented pupil, the Mozzarella Monks bowed deeply to him. Luno bowed in return.

"So this is Planet Formaggio," Luno said, looking around.

"It isn't actually *planet*," Due added. "It's more like a giant cheese ball we made."

Then Due turned and shouted at one of the monks, "Nove! Quit eating the planet!"

"Sorry," Nove said, wiping his chin.

Tre asked Luno how he was able to find Formaggio, when the monks took such great lengths to stay hidden.

"Why?" Chooch asked. "Don't you *want* to be found?"

"No!" replied Master Uno. "Because every Tom, Dick, and Luno will start showing up!"

"Hey," said Chooch. "*His* name is Luno!"

"See what I mean?" asked Master Uno.

Clive explained that they arrived via wormhole. Chooch assured them that there weren't any space worms in it.

Luno asked Tre, who seemed to be the least loopy of the monks, who they were hiding *from*.

"Vlactron," said Tre.

The Mozzarella Monks shuddered at the sound of the name. Otto fainted and had to be revived with a piece of Limburger.

"You mean *Vlactron's* real, *too*?" Luno asked. "And still *alive*?"

Tre nodded grimly.

Luno explained to Clive and Chooch his father told him that years ago, Vlactron tried to steal the Golden Anchovy from Solaro, then Luno stopped mid-sentence and turned to the monks.

"And the *Golden Anchovy*?" Luno asked.

The Mozzarella Monks smiled and nodded, *Yes, it's real, too.*

"Why didn't Vlactron *just* take the Golden Anchovy from Solaro if he wanted it so badly?" Luno asked.

Tre explained that the Golden Anchovy could not be taken, but only willingly *given*, otherwise it would die.

"'But if you steal it,'" Luno recited the rhyme to himself, "'you hereby cause the Golden Anchovy to die.' Wow. I haven't thought of that in years."

Tre went on to explain that Vlactron threatened the monks to convince Solaro to give it to *him*, which was when the Monks left Planet Formaggio, went into hiding, and made Formaggio2, where they currently were. As far as Tre knew, Vlactron was still looking for the Golden Anchovy to this very day.

"So where's the Golden Anchovy *now*?" Luno asked.

No one knew, but Due explained that the name of the one who would someday find it had been written on the ancient Stilton Stones.

"But unfortunately, they were carved out of cheese,"

said Due. "And *Nove* here ate them before we could read the name on the tablet!"

"I said I was *sorry!*" Nove shouted.

"They were over a thousand years old!" said Due.

"What can I say?" said Nove. "I love aged Stilton!"

"Hmmm. Is that Vlactron fellow the one with that pizzeria?" Master Uno asked, scratching his chin. "You know—Quasar? Quotient? Quahog?"

"*QUANTUM?!*" Luno shouted. "You mean *Vlactron* runs *Quantum*, the biggest, most-cutthroat pizzeria chain in the galaxy?"

Luno frantically paced back and forth waving his arms around, ranting about what would happen if the most dangerous alien got his hands on the most powerful pizza topping. Zorgoochi Intergalactic Pizza wouldn't stand a chance! With the protection of the Golden Anchovy, *nothing* could stop Vlactron from destroying his parents' pizzeria. He would be *invincible*!

Then Luno fell to ground, panting.

Master Uno looked up at the setting suns and then to the rest of the Mozzarella Monks. Without a word, they stepped over Luno and started toward the mountain.

"*Wait* a minute," said Luno, getting up. "What are you *doing*?"

"It's time to go," said Master Uno.

"But you have to find the Golden Anchovy!" said Luno. "You have to stop *Vlactron!*"

"No, we don't," said Master Uno.

"Well, if *you* don't, then who *will*?" Luno asked.

"*You*, young Zorgoochi," said Master Uno. "Come. It is time you learned the Whey of Life."

PART 2

CHAPTER NINE

The Whey of Life

The monks silently climbed the foothills as Luno followed them, his head spinning from having just learned that the supposed fairy tales his father had told him his entire childhood were actually real. The most vicious alien in the universe owned the biggest pizza chain in the galaxy and it would be up to Luno to defeat him. Sure, this would save Zorgoochi Intergalactic Pizza, but Luno had no idea if or how he would even do this.

Also, he really didn't want to die.

And what did all of this have to do with cheese making?

Clive trailed behind, gathering information, contentedly scanning rocks and plants with his device.

Chooch, however, was getting nervous. The suns were setting and he was afraid of the dark. He held Luno's hand tight, causing a few of his knuckles to crack.

"Our monastery is a treacherous ten-mile hike into the Muenster Mountains," said Master Uno, motioning to a lone peak off in the distance.

"Why didn't you just build your monastery over *there*?" Luno asked, pointing back at the flat expanse behind them where he parked the pod.

The monks angrily turned to Nove and then Quattro smacked him upside the head.

"*See?*" said Quattro. "Even *he* said we should've built it over *there!*"

"I said I was *sorry*," Nove grumbled.

Luno scrambled over the rocks, pulling Chooch along and trying to keep up with the monks as they marched ahead.

"Look," said Luno, catching up to Master Uno, "thanks for the offer to show me how to make cheese, but I really think I should get back to my deliveries."

"Then you should inform your feet," said Uno, "because you're still following us."

"But I really can't stay here," said Luno. "I need to get back out there."

"There is no 'here' *or* 'out there,'" said Master Uno. "There is no difference, young Zorgoochi."

Tre recommended Luno accept Master Uno's offer

to train him in the art of cheese making, but Luno couldn't see how it would help defeat Vlactron.

"Well, it couldn't *hurt*," said Master Uno.

Luno was concerned that he was already going to be late for his next delivery, but Master Uno assured him that his training would take no time at all.

"Well, exactly how long *will* it take?" Luno asked.

"Exactly as long as it'll take for you to learn how to make cheese," said Master Uno. "*And not a second more.*"

"That did *not* answer my question," Luno grumbled.

"Well, then don't question my answer," said Master Uno.

Chooch announced that the reason they flew into the wormhole in the first place was because Luno was running away from Vlactron's delivery ships.

Luno glared at Chooch, but then hung his head in shame.

"Ah, sometimes the better part of valor is discretion," said Master Uno, giving Luno a consoling pat on the back.

"What does *that* mean?" asked Chooch.

"I'm not sure," said Master Uno. "But it sure *sounds* good, doesn't it?"

"I believe what Master Uno is saying," said Tre, "is that there are times when being cautious is wiser than being courageous."

"Young Zorgoochi, you may not have been running *away* from something," said Master Uno, "as much as *toward* something."

The rest of the journey was made without a word. However, there was a full-on debate inside Luno's head. Why *him*? Why did *he* have to take down Vlactron and not the monks? There were nine of them and only *one* of him! And what about *Dad*? *He* should do it. He was an adult!

Luno wanted all this to go away. Maybe if he didn't do anything, it would resolve itself on its own. Maybe Vlactron would never even find the Golden Anchovy. And even if he *did* and used its powers and protection in order to destroy Zorgoochi Intergalactic Pizza and become the most popular pizzeria in the Mezzaluna Galaxy, maybe it wouldn't be so bad living in a galaxy dominated by Quantum. Maybe the universe would blow up and he wouldn't have to deal with any of this. Maybe . . .

"Welcome to the Fromage Friary," said Master Uno, pushing open the squeaky gate to the Mozzarella Monk's mountaintop monastery.

A bright moon shone down on a very large, but simple structure, quite the opposite picture Luno had in his head when his father told him about the monastery so many years ago. He always imagined a grand, ornate palace with carved columns, mosaic floors, and some sort of cheese shrine in its center. This looked more like a barn. And it smelled like one, too.

Luno's brain was buzzing with fear, anxiety, and panic, but mostly fatigue. He was led to what he surmised in the darkness to be a stable by the faint animal grunts and rank odor.

Regardless, Luno collapsed onto a pile of hay and immediately fell asleep.

In what seemed like only a few seconds, Luno's eyes fluttered open. The harsh morning sunlight made him squint. A massive hairy gray tongue was licking his face. Its owner was a giant smelly creature, which burped death breath up Luno's nose.

"Ah, I see you've met Bessie," said Tre, offering his hand to help Luno to his feet. "It's time for breakfast. I hope you like cheese!"

"Do you have anything *else*?" Luno asked, picking straw out of his hair and wiping the disgusting, sticky animal slobber from his face.

"Um," said Tre, "No."

As Luno walked past Bessie, she wrapped her tail around him, pulling him back and licking him some more.

"Hey!" said Tre as he unwound her tail. "I think she likes you!"

"Great," Luno muttered, wiping off more drool.

Tre swung open the door to the monastery and

Luno walked in. As he was bathed in the aroma of warm delicious cheese, a serene calm suddenly washed over him. Even though it was only a few short hours ago, Luno couldn't imagine how he could've possibly been worried about any of the things that had been plaguing him the night before.

At the far end of the cavernous room was a stone hearth with a massive bubbling caldron hanging over a fire, and in the middle was a long wooden table where the monks, as well as Clive and Chooch, were talking and eating.

Luno sat down and greeted everyone. Sei placed a bowl in front of Luno and Sette filled it with a ladleful of warm lumpy cheese.

"Thank you," said Luno. Sei and Sette nodded mutely.

Luno asked if they had taken a vow of silence.

"No, they claimed they've said everything they've needed to say," explained Due. "Now if only *Nove* here would do the same!"

Nove rolled his eyes and went back to his breakfast.

Luno looked over at Otto, who was not eating at all, and asked if he was fasting.

"Oh, *him*? He can't eat cheese," said Due. "He's lactose intolerant, but we let him hang around us anyway."

Clive was having an intellectually stimulating conversation with Cinque about the chemistry of cheese making. Next to him, Chooch's face was buried in a giant bowl of fresh cottage cheese.

"They said I can eat all I want!" said Chooch, coming up for air. "This is the greatest place *ever*! Can we live here?"

As Chooch plunged his face back into his bowl, Luno dug into his breakfast.

It was as if he'd never tasted cheese before. Sure, the homemade mozzarella his father made at the pizzeria was delicious, but it was nothing like *this*. Luno could actually taste the earthy flavor of the grass Bessie had eaten.

Before he knew it, he was scraping the bottom of the bowl with his spoon.

"Time to begin your training, young Zorgoochi," Master Uno said, standing up.

Luno dutifully followed him out of the monastery and into a nearby field.

"Dig a hole exactly five feet deep," Master Uno said, handing him a shovel. Luno obediently began to dig.

He sweated, struggled, and strained under the hot suns as Master Uno sat cross-legged under a tree in the cool shade, watching him intently. Luno had no idea why he would need to dig a hole to make cheese, but figured Master Uno did, so Luno continued to dig, even though it made no sense to him.

After hours of toiling, the top of the hole was even

with the tip of Luno's nose, so he knew it was five feet deep. He climbed out.

"I'm done, Master Uno," Luno said, panting, dirty, and exhausted.

Master Uno did not answer. He just blankly stared ahead.

"Master Uno?" said Luno, but there still was no response. "Um, Master *Uno*?" Luno said a bit louder.

"Hmmm?" Master Uno asked, and then yawned. "I must've fallen asleep. I sleep with my eyes open, by the way."

Master Uno stood up and stretched, then sauntered over to the hole and looked in.

"Nice hole," Master Uno commented. "Okay, now fill it in."

"Fill it *in*?" Luno asked. "Then why did I dig it?"

"Oh, I just like watching people dig holes," Master Uno said, walking away.

"Then this was all just a big waste of time?" Luno huffed. "Why did I listen to you? I *knew* it made no sense!"

"Ah! Very good!" said Master Uno. "You've learned Lesson Number One—trust your instincts."

Luno sighed.

An hour later, Master Uno and Luno were sitting cross-legged, side by side on the very peak of Mount Muenster. He instructed Luno to close his eyes.

"See the cheese you want to make," said Master Uno.

Luno closed his eyes. He shifted and wiggled, trying to picture the perfect cheese, but what would it look like? He'd seen cheese every day of his life at the pizzeria and it all pretty much looked the same to him.

Dozens of cheese wheels, cheese balls, and even cheese sticks floated around in Luno's brain. For a long time he had no idea what he was looking for until he noticed a hunk hovering far off in the distance of his imagination. Luno focused and drew it closer. It was not entirely round or even square, kind of lopsided really, but he somehow knew, *this was his cheese.*

Luno's eyes popped open.

"I think I understand, Master Uno," Luno said. "I first need to *visualize* the cheese in order to bring it into existence, right?"

"Oh, I was just asking if you wanted to use a round or square cheese mold," said Master Uno, "but let's go with what you just said."

Luno sighed.

Master Uno explained that the next step was to gather the ingredients.

"Everything you see around us, the monastery, those lemon trees over there, the Mozzarella Monks, even you and me," Master Uno said to Luno as they approached an orchard, "this is all an *illusion.*"

"Huh?" asked Luno. "What does *that* mean?"

"For example," Master Uno said, picking up a rock, "you only *think* this is real."

Then Master Uno dropped the rock on Luno's foot. *Ouch!*

"You only *think* the pain is real," he continued. "But pain and fear and that rock, like everything else, young Zorgoochi, are merely *illusions*. They don't truly exist."

"So I *imagined* that it hurt," said Luno, rubbing his foot, "and everything around me?"

"Exactly! You must remember that none of this is real and nothing can hurt you, unless you *let* it."

Master Uno picked up a much larger different colored rock and said, "Trust me."

Luno grit his teeth, anticipating the pain to come.

"Most live their lives in fear," Master Uno said as he dropped the rock on Luno's foot. It softly bounced off.

Luno picked it up. It was light as a feather. Master Uno grinned and picked up another rock. Luno smiled as Master Uno dropped it on his foot.

"Ouch!" Luno cried. That one was heavy. And painful.

"There's fear of pain, fear of failure, fear of the unknown, fear of someone dropping a heavy rock on your foot, and in your case, fear of *Vlactron*, but fear, like everything else, is merely an *illusion*," he said, handing Luno a basket. "And I want you to remember while filling this with lemons that you will not be free from fear until you have transcended your ego and let go of this reality."

Whatever, Luno shrugged.

Luno approached a tree and reached for a lemon, then pulled it off the branch. Before it hit the bottom of the basket, Luno's eyes were crossed and he was gasping for breath.

"Gak!" Luno struggled to unclench the tree branch wrapped around his throat. Another branch grabbed his feet and turned him upside down. As the tree shook him by the ankles, Luno could see Master Uno waving to him from a safe distance.

"Remember!" smiled Master Uno. "It's all an illusion!"

Oddly enough, this was not the first time Luno found himself in a situation like this. It wasn't much different from wrestling the Cosmic Calamari that guarded the Sea Garlic in the giant tank in the kitchen back at the pizzeria.

He wriggled free of the branches.

"Hah!" Luno shouted, triumphantly holding up a lemon, but was soon scooped up by a tree behind him and had to wrestle his way out once again, snatching another lemon in the process. This went on for about an hour, until Luno was crawling back to Master Uno, battered and exhausted, dragging a full basket.

"So? Did you remember that it was all in your mind, young Zorgoochi?" Master Uno asked.

"I think I still need to work on that." Luno sighed as he collapsed facedown in the grass.

They entered the barn and the moment Bessie saw Luno, her ears perked up and she lovingly wrapped her tail around him and licked him passionately. *Blech!* Luno somehow preferred the psychotic lemon trees to this.

Once her tail was unraveled, Luno was instructed

in the art of milking, which was made all the more difficult by Bessie trying to lick him. Luno learned quickly, mostly because he wanted it to be over with as soon as possible.

Finally finished, he presented a giant bucket of milk to Master Uno.

"Very good, young Zorgoochi," said Master Uno. "Now, the last ingredient is *salt*."

After a day of pointlessly digging and then filling a hole, fighting angry lemon trees, and then being covered in disgusting alien spit, Luno finally cracked.

"*Now* what?" Luno shouted. "Go into a salt mine with a pickaxe and dig out a hunk of salt, lug it back here, and grind it myself in order to attain higher consciousness or something?"

"No," Master Uno said, calmly reaching for a nearby shelf. "We keep it in this saltshaker here."

Luno sighed.

He lugged the sloshing bucket of milk and the basket of lemons to the cheese making room as Master Uno trailed behind with the saltshaker.

"Wake me up when you've squeezed the juice from the lemons," yawned Master Uno.

He did as he was told and, with a twisted, puckered, quivering hand, poked Master Uno awake.

Luno was then instructed to pour the milk into a caldron in the center of the room and to light a fire beneath it. Master Uno handed him a spoon the size of a canoe oar and told him to stir the milk and not to stop.

Luno never thought much about stirring, but according to Master Uno, he had been doing it incorrectly his whole life. No matter how much Luno thought he was following Master Uno's instructions exactly, he *still* told Luno he was doing it wrong.

After an hour, Luno's arms were numb, but fortunately, he was used to this from the thousands of hours he spent with Roog back at the pizzeria trying to perfect the Zorgoochi Pizza Toss.

The milk finally began to bubble around the edges of the caldron and once it was at a full boil, Master Uno asked Luno to douse the fire and pour in the lemon juice.

"That *can't* be right," said Luno. "The lemon juice will curdle the milk!"

"Sometimes the *right* thing isn't always the logical thing," said Master Uno, "but you do it anyway."

Luno put out the fire and, just to prove him wrong, dumped the lemon juice into the milk. Sure enough, the milk separated and big lumps began to form.

"See?" Luno said.

"The curds are the solid part," explained Master Uno, once again handing Luno the giant spoon. "And the whey is the liquid part."

It was disgusting to look at, but Luno stirred,

trying to do it exactly as Master Uno showed him, but he still wasn't mixing it thoroughly enough for him.

"*Be* the cheese," Master Uno said. "Imagine yourself as one of those curds separating from the whey."

As Luno peered into the caldron, Master Uno pushed him in.

Luno thrashed around the warm whey, futilely grasping at the curds and the slippery edges of the caldron, churning the milk.

"Ah, that's much *better*!" said Master Uno. "You're really mixing it up nicely now!"

"I'm also *drowning*!" Luno gurgled.

"Yes, well, that's to be expected," said Master Uno, watching Luno flail about. "Remember, young Zorgoochi, this is all an illusion. You only *think* you're drowning."

"No." Luno gulped, as he went down for the third time. "I'm pretty sure I'm drowning."

"Just as the curds separate from the whey and float to the surface, young Zorgoochi," crooned Master Uno, "you must separate yourself from your fears to ascend to a higher consciousness."

After a few moments, Luno gave up and sunk to the bottom, holding his breath, something he learned to do from Roog "accidentally" knocking him into a vat of clam sauce (with vicious snapping clams no less), an Olympic-pool-size stewpot full of tomato sauce, as well

as into one of the ponds behind the pizzeria full of attacking algae.

Luno rested on the bottom of the caldron and
watched the cheese curds lazily pulling away from the
whey.

After a few moments, he began to gently float to the
surface.

Master Uno reached for Luno's hand and helped
him out.

"Do you understand what I mean *now*?" Master Uno
asked a dripping wet Luno.

"I-I think so," coughed Luno.

"Good," said Master Uno.
"Now maybe you can explain
it to *me*. I'm a little fuzzy on
the whole thing."

Luno sighed.

They then poured the contents of the caldron through gigantic cheesecloth, separating the lumpy curds from the whey. Luno added salt and dumped the curds into a cheese mold the size of a suitcase.

Lugging the massive mold, Luno followed Master Uno as he entered an opening at the foot of the mountain. It was cold, dark, and quiet down in the Camembert Caverns beneath the monastery. Luno could see his breath.

"Now you must stay with the cheese until it cools," said Master Uno, walking away. "And remember—"

"Yeah, yeah," said Luno. "It's all an illusion."

"Oh, I was actually going to say try not to freeze to death," said Master Uno. "But let's go with what you just said."

The cavern was cold and the cheese was still warm, so Luno snuggled up next to it and fell asleep.

While he slept, the cheese slowly chilled, leaving Luno shivering, but a few hours later, a shaft of warm light from the rising suns fell on his face. Luno slowly floated up toward semiconsciousness.

You already know what to do, Luno. His father's voice echoed in his head. *Now do it.*

Luno's eyes popped open.

Everything was clear.

He knew that if he didn't face Vlactron, he would

spend the rest of his life hiding from him. *Or worse*, Vlactron would eventually find the Golden Anchovy and take over the galaxy forever.

Luno knew that the only thing stopping him was fear and *that* was just an illusion, just like everything else.

At least he really really *hoped* so.

"I think I understand now, Master Uno," Luno said, entering the monastery, lugging the giant cheese. Master Uno, Clive, Chooch, and the monks stood up.

"And what is *that*?" asked Master Uno.

"I must separate the curds from the whey," Luno said, struggling to put the cheese on the dining table. "And face Vlactron. My fear, just like everything else, is just an illusion."

"Your training is complete, young Zorgoochi," announced Master Uno.

Chooch jumped up and down and cheered, "Group hug!"

Once Luno and everyone else were released from Chooch's loving yet viselike hug, Luno asked, "So have I *really* learned the Whey of Life, Master Uno?"

"What're you asking *me* for?" said Master Uno. "I'm just an illusion."

Luno sighed.

After a breakfast of (what else?) cheese, they descended the mountain.

By the time they reached the foothills, Chooch had already eaten the ten-pound wheel of Gouda the monks had given him as a going-away gift and Clive had almost completed a new theory about the physics of cheese making.

As they made their way to the delivery pod, Clive asked Master Uno if he and Luno and Chooch had traveled through the wormhole and found Formaggio2, then why hadn't others?

"Because no one would be stupid enough to fly straight into a black hole?" Nove asked.

"For once, Nove," said Master Uno, "you are correct."

Luno thought about this as they walked to the pod, but then stopped dead in his tracks.

"The fan belt!" he said, smacking himself on the forehead. "I still have to fix it!"

"Oh, I took care of *that*," said Cinque.

Confused, Luno turned to Master Uno.

"I told you *I* didn't know anything about engines." Master Uno smiled. "I never said *he* didn't."

After another one of Chooch's painful group hugs, Luno climbed up to the hatch.

"Say cheese!" said Otto.

Luno looked around for a camera, but no one was holding one.

"Oh, we just like saying cheese!" explained Otto.

"CHEESE!" everyone shouted.

Luno stopped himself as he was climbing into the pod.

"Wait a minute!" Luno called to Master Uno. "I got here through a wormhole. I have no idea how to get back!"

"The appropriate course to take would be back through the same wormhole," said Clive.

"And so you shall!" announced Master Uno. "The boys and I are going to open it for you."

"How are you able to create a hole in the spacetime continuum?" Clive asked.

"By performing Tele-Swiss-Kinesis," said Due.

"How do you think we make the holes in Swiss cheese? It's all mind over Muenster," Master Uno said. "Now buckle up!"

Once Clive and Chooch bid the monks good-bye and were all in the delivery pod, Luno popped his head out before closing the hatch and waved.

"Remember, young Zorgoochi, it's all an illusion," said Master Uno. "But then again, I could be entirely wrong!"

Luno sighed, closed the hatch, and watched the Mozzarella Monks through the windshield as they sat in a circle cross-legged on the ground with their eyes closed.

Suddenly, the sky grew dark and the wind kicked up, blowing Master Uno's beard sideways. Luno, Clive, and Chooch buckled their seat belts as a massive black hole began to form right above them.

They lifted off and Luno aimed the delivery pod straight into the wormhole.

Then everything went black.

CHAPTER TEN

Have an Ice Day!

Luno woke to the sharp *ping* of Quantum delivery ships' fire ricocheting off the delivery pod.

"Quantum ship at 6:15!" Chooch shouted.

Luno looked down at the clock and sure enough it was 6:15, not only the same date they entered the worm-hole, but the *exact same time* as well! Master Uno was right. *It took no time at all.*

Luno had to shake those Quantum ships off his tail, so there wasn't time to contemplate the weirdness of the universe. A convenient cosmic cloudbank lay ahead, so with Master Uno's *Sometimes the better part of valor is discretion* ringing in his ears, Luno leaned forward and flew straight into it.

The cloudbank's molecular density increased the deeper Luno flew, and the deeper he flew, the fewer Quantum ships followed, until he couldn't see any more following him. Luno figured that they had better things to do, like dominating the galaxy, rather than chasing him.

Luno decided to wait awhile before heading off to Planet Freezorg, his last delivery. Through the cosmic mist, he saw vague silhouettes slowly moving about. Were they vicious space sharks about to go in for the kill? A collection of intelligent particles that ate pizza delivery boys? Space mirages?

He carefully navigated through the dense fog guided only by the pod's instruments, which was difficult enough, but made more so by Chooch clutching Luno's legs in panic, muttering something about his seat cushion also being a flotation device. Also distracting was Clive's dissertation on particle density, which he dryly delivered, completely unaware of the potential dangers surrounding them.

As the pod crept forward, the mist thinned and the shapes became clear. Luno saw that they weren't ferocious creatures after all. They were just delivery ships from other family-owned pizzerias, like Zorgoochi's—Famous Fazul's, Mezzaluna, and di Mension, among others—and they were doing the same thing he was doing: hiding from Quantum Pizza.

Then it dawned on Luno. Vlactron wasn't trying to just run Zorgoochi Intergalactic Pizza out of business, he was trying to run *all* pizzerias out of business, so Quantum would be the only one left in the entire galaxy. Maybe even the *universe*!

Luno decided he'd hidden in the cloudbank long enough. He had to make that third delivery or his father would clobber him, so he shifted the pod into gear and started making his way out onto the main spaceway.

"Hey," said Chooch, "they're *following* us!"

Luno looked at the rearview screen and gulped hard. Sure enough, the other ships were lining up behind him as if he were bravely leading them into battle against Vlactron for the freedom of pizza in the galaxy. Luno's epiphany of separating himself from his fears he had back on Formaggio2 quickly evaporated and the threat from Quantum didn't feel at all like an illusion, but very real. He suddenly felt weak, small, and afraid.

Once he was positive there were no Quantum ships around, Luno slammed down on the accelerator, and left the other ships in the cosmic dust.

Luno's train of thought was suddenly derailed by a nudge from Chooch's big metal elbow.

"Oooh!" Chooch shouted, pointing out the windshield at the glistening white sphere in the distance. "Look at the giant snowball!"

"That's not a snowball," Luno said, squinting. "It's Planet Freezorg."

"You are *both* right," said Clive. "Freezorg is indeed a planet, but made entirely of snow and ice."

Within moments, they were zooming over the icy wasteland looking for a place to land. As they cleared a frozen mountain peak, Luno saw in the distance that, once again, a Quantum delivery ship was taking off having already intercepted the order.

Beaten out of another delivery!

Luno drew a big sigh as he touched down on Planet Freezorg's frozen surface.

Soon Luno, Clive, and Chooch were forging across

the barren tundra to find the person who ordered the pizza. "I *gotta* get paid for this delivery."

Luno looked around at the miles of frozen nothingness in every direction. He could see his sigh rise up in a little cloud of steam. Meanwhile Clive calculated precisely how long it would take for them to freeze to death.

"Hellooo!" Luno shouted.

Suddenly, the snow began to rumble and crack beneath their feet! Then a hunk of ice rose up, forming into a towering ice creature!

"Hey, man," said the ice creature, bending down and straightening his frozen glasses to get a good look at Luno. "Who are *you*?"

"I'm Luno from Zorgoochi Intergalactic Pizza with a large pizza for"—Luno squinted at the receipt—"*Frosto Snowski?*"

"Hey, gang!" Frosto shouted. "It's *another* pizza guy!"

The ground trembled and three more ice creatures rose up from the ground.

Frosto explained that their pizza had already been delivered. By Quantum.

After being chased, shot at, nearly eaten by giant mushroom creatures, almost burned to a crisp, and nearly drowned in a caldron of cheese curds, Luno did the only logical thing he could think of.

He cried.

As Luno sat on the frozen ground and sobbed, he told the Freezorgs that it was his first day as a delivery boy for his family's pizzeria and how Quantum Pizza had been beating him to all of his deliveries. He messed up the first two and was pretty sure his dad would be mad at him for not getting paid and never trust him again and would not only have to make the pizzas, but deliver them, too, and after 200 years, Zorgoochi Intergalactic Pizza would probably go out of business and it would be all his fault and . . . and . . .

The Freezorgs felt sorry for Luno so they gave him

a hug, but because of Luno's tears, they all stuck together like a wet tongue on an ice cube.

Even though he wasn't made out of ice, the Freezorgs liked Luno and agreed to pay for the pizza. Luno thanked them. One payment was better than none.

Then Frosto introduced Luno to his chilly chums Snowy Joey, Floe, and Sheldon, who all started chanting, "Piz-*za*! Piz-*za*! Piz-*za*!" They twitched, jumped, and waved their arms, which Luno took to be dancing.

Luno opened Chooch's oven, sending out a blast of heat. He handed Frosto the pizza, but before he could take it, Frosto's hands began to melt and within moments, he was a soupy puddle, then a cloud of steam.

Before the rest of the Freezorgs could turn to slush, Luno quickly slammed Chooch's oven door shut.

"Sorry about that," Luno said sheepishly.

"I guess I forgot to tell you the pizza should've been *frozen*," said Frosto, as he refroze back into his former frosty self.

Luno handed the now-cold pizza to Frosto, who paid him with a handful of little frozen coins. Luno gratefully put them in his pocket.

"You know what would cheer you up?" Floe asked. "A snowball fight!"

The Freezorgs cheered, "Snowball *fight*! Snowball *fight*!"

"No thanks," Luno said. "I really should get back to the pizzeria."

"C'*mon*!" said Snowy Joey. "Don't be a slush-a-roo!"

No matter how many times they called Luno a slush-a-roo, Luno refused to join in on the fun, so the Freezorgs went off to have a snowball fight without him.

Luno turned and started back to the delivery pod. "C'mon, guys, lets—"

But turned to see Chooch happily running off with the Freezorgs.

Great.

"Pardon me, Mr. Zorgoochi," said Clive. "I would like to conduct a scientific study of this 'snowball fight.'"

Luno sighed. *Okay, but just for a minute!*

He watched as they all had a blast throwing snowballs at one another. Even Clive had a good time. Well, as much as a super-intelligent gamma-ray-infused mutant bulb of garlic could, calculating the average weight and velocity of each snowball.

Meanwhile, Luno got colder and colder waiting for them.

Luno cracked off a frozen drip from the end of his nose. He could barely feel his hands as he rubbed them together. His feet felt like two blocks of ice. He was shivering and his eyebrows were starting to freeze, reminding him of the time Roog locked him in the freezer and how moving around had made him warmer. He didn't want to admit it, but he wished he'd listened to his mother and brought a sweater.

Luno decided to join in the snowball fight, but only as a means of survival.

"Hey, dudes!" Frosto shouted as Luno walked up. "Look who decided to finally join us!"

Fzzzooom!

Three glistening snowballs zoomed right toward Luno's head! He ducked the same way he ducked Roog throwing imperfect meatballs at him.

Luno ran as fast as he could to the safety of Chooch's fort as snowballs whizzed past his ears.

Calling on his meatball-making abilities, Luno showed Chooch how to make the perfect snowball by packing it super tight and perfectly round. Then he demonstrated the best way to throw it by pulling his arm way back *before* he stood up, so he'd be vulnerable to attack only for a split second.

Thwack!

It *worked*! Sheldon got it right between the eyes and fell over giggling.

Luno pelted the Freezorgs with an armful of snowballs as he deftly dodged more snowballs coming at him from all directions. Clive followed close behind, pecking away at his little device, making a thorough analysis of the geometric dimensions of the spheres of sub-32-degree H_2O flying over his head.

Snow flew everywhere and soon Luno flopped backward, sweating, panting, and giggling.

"Snow angels!" Floe shouted as she fell back and waved her arms and legs. They all agreed that Chooch's was the best snow angel they'd ever seen. Clive took a holograph for further study.

"Who wants to go home and have some pizza?" asked Frosto.

Luno looked around at the frozen wasteland.

"Where's *home*?" he asked.

"It's right *here*," said Frosto. "Watch!"

All four Freezorgs stood in a big circle and raised their arms. The ground rumbled and massive hunks of snow shot out from the ground, creating an icy cloud.

After a few moments, the swirling mist lifted, revealing a giant complex, glistening structure. It was the most beautiful thing Luno had ever seen.

"C'mon in!" called Frosto.

CHAPTER ELEVEN

Three Stages of Matter Really Matter

"This is the coolest place *ever!*" Luno said as they all walked into the giant glittering construction.

"It's so *pretty!*" said Chooch.

"It is the most exquisite star tetrahedron I've ever seen," said Clive, who knew a good polygon when he saw one.

Floe hung an ice disco ball, Snowy Joey passed out snow cones, and Sheldon cranked up the groovy tunes. The Freezorgs twitched, jumped, and waved their arms and Luno was pretty sure they were dancing. They weren't very good, but it didn't seem to bother them. In fact, they were all having such a good time, Chooch joined in and did The Robot. Sheldon did The Swim, but got seasick.

"It is getting late, Mr. Zorgoochi," Clive shouted over the music. "We should leave."

Luno couldn't hear him; he was too busy twitching, jumping, and waving his arms around with the rest of them. He wasn't a very good dancer, either.

"Who wants pizza?" someone shouted and they all thought it was the best idea ever. The Freezorgs gave one another high-fives. Unfortunately, most of them missed and smacked one another on the head, but they didn't seem to care.

Sheldon walked up carrying the frozen pizza and some sort of gadget, made of snow, just like everything else on Freezorg. He put the pizza inside it and pressed a button.

"What *is* this?" Luno asked, peering into the little window and watching the pizza turn round and round.

"It's a *macrowave*," Frosto explained. "*Micro*waves excite molecules and make stuff hot, well, this slows them down and makes stuff *ice cold!*"

Ping!

Frosto pulled out the pizza and cracked off a slice

for everyone. Luno bit into a piece, almost breaking a tooth.

"This place is incredible," said Luno through a mouthful of frozen pizza, looking up at the glistening crystal structure overhead.

Then he noticed what time it was and all the frosty fun he just had seemed to melt away. Luno had made his deliveries and it was time to head back to the pizzeria.

They reluctantly made their way to the delivery pod.

Then Luno climbed up onto the wing.

"Well," Luno said awkwardly. "I guess I'll see you guys around."

The Freezorgs shouted good-bye and invited them to come back real soon. Luno smiled and thanked them for paying for the pizza.

He climbed into the pod, but then popped his head back out.

"And thanks for a great time."

Luno closed the hatch, slid into the driver's seat, and switched on the engine. As he ground the pod into gear and lifted off, Luno looked at the rearview screen and watched the Freezorgs frantically waving.

As they got smaller and smaller, Luno thought about how mad his father was going to be when he told him he only got paid for one pizza. If it was possible, Luno's brow knitted even more when he thought of Vlactron.

Should I tell Dad? Should I do nothing? Should I—

"Fifteen minutes until impact," Clive muttered to himself as he pecked away at his device.

"Huh?" Luno asked. "*What* impact?"

"Why, the impact of the meteors with Planet Freezorg when they pass through its orbital path," said Clive distractedly.

Luno's head spun, but not because another Quantum Pizza delivery ship crossed their path.

"Meteors?" Chooch shrieked. "Let's get out of here before we're all destroyed!"

"Matter cannot be destroyed, only *transformed*," corrected Clive. "And in the case of H_2O, there is liquid, solid, and gas, however—"

"*Not* a good time for a science lesson, Clive," said Luno, looking at Planet Freezorg, now the size of a snowball in the rearview screen.

A wave of fear washed over Luno as he squeezed the gearshift. Every muscle was aching for him to slam into high gear and floor it out of there.

Luno turned to see Clive pointing to the screen on his device and his mouth moving and Chooch rolling around on the floor, clutching his head and shouting something, but he couldn't hear what they were saying. In fact, he couldn't hear anything at all, except his own heart beating.

Luno had no idea why his thoughts suddenly turned

to cheese making, but when he saw curds separating from whey in his mind's eye, he understood and became calm.

You already know what to do, Geo's voice echoed in his head. *Now* do *it.*

Luno pulled back on the steering stick, pecked a few buttons, and shifted the pod into reverse.

"What are you *doing*, Luno?" Chooch whimpered. "The *meteors* are coming!"

"I'm going *back*," said Luno. "To save the Freezorgs."

"I do not understand, Mr. Zorgoochi," said Clive. "This does not make sense."

Luno ignored him.

Moments later, the pod touched down in the snow and Luno emerged from the hatch. The Freezorgs curiously surrounded him, asking if he forgot to use the bathroom before he left.

"I got some bad news," Luno announced. "A bunch of meteors are heading straight for Freezorg!"

"We have bad news, too," said Snowy Joey. "Sheldon lost his retainer."

"Didn't you hear me?" Luno smacked his forehead. "You're all going to be DESTROYED!"

"As I previously stated, Mr. Zorgoochi," sniffed Clive, "matter cannot be destroyed, only *transformed*."

The Freezorgs looked at one another, then twitched,

jumped, and waved their arms, but *this* time they weren't dancing. Sheldon immediately got a case of nervous hiccups.

Luno knew he had to save them, but there was just a small problem.

He had no idea *how*.

Whenever Chooch was scared, he ate pizza. He also ate pizza when he was happy, sad, sleepy, or hungry.

Chooch opened the door of the pizza oven in his chest and pulled out a slice and when Luno saw the blast of heat melt Snowy Joey's fingers, he got an idea.

"Matter cannot be destroyed, only *transformed*, right?" Luno asked Clive.

"Yes, Mr. Zorgoochi," said Clive. "That is correct."

Luno turned up the temperature on Chooch's oven and yanked the door wide-open, blasting the Freezorgs with heat.

"Hey, man!" Frosto shouted. "That is totally *un-cool*!"

"Exactly!" said Luno. "In fact, it's gonna get down-right *hot* in a minute!"

"But you'll *melt* us!" said Floe, pointing a dripping finger.

"Don't worry, I know what I'm doing!" smiled Luno. "I got a C- in science!"

Puzzled, Chooch and Clive watched the Freezorgs

turn into soupy puddles, and then the rest of the sur-face of the planet quickly turn from ice to slush.

Keeping his oven door wide-open, Luno sat Chooch on the top of the delivery pod. As the melting slush grew deeper, he and Clive boarded the pod before there was nothing left to stand on.

With the delivery pod now hovering over an ocean of melted ice and snow, the water then began to trans-form into a giant planet-size bank of fog.

"Quite ingenious, Mr. Zorgoochi," observed Clive. "Now that the planet has transformed from solid to liq-uid to gas, the meteors cannot collide with it, but merely pass through."

"And once the meteors pass, the Freezorgs and the rest of the planet can be refrozen," said Luno. "At least I *think* so."

CLUNK! CLUNK! CLUNK!

Chooch pounded on the hatch and shouted that the meteors were on their way and to please let him in now! Luno opened the hatch and Chooch fell to the floor.

CLANK!

Freezorg was now just a collection of microscopic water molecules huddled together in space. Somewhere in there was Frosto, Snowy Joey, Floe, and Sheldon.

That's what Luno was counting on anyway.

Through the mist, Luno saw giant fiery boulders hurtling toward them and slammed the pod into gear.

"Hang *on!*" Luno shouted, as he stomped his foot down on the gas pedal and zoomed them out of the meteors' path.

Once at a safe distance, Luno, Clive, and Chooch watched the blazing meteors moving closer and closer until . . .

VROOOOOM!

Luno suddenly found himself plastered against the wall, helplessly watching everything in the cabin spin out of control!

"To fasten your seat belt," said Chooch, "insert the metal fittings one into the other, and . . ."

The pod's piercing emergency siren filled Luno's ears as he crawled his way back to the pilot's seat. He yanked the seat belt hard and snapped it closed. The blinking buttons on the control panel made him queasy, but he found the right button and the spinning stopped.

"Is everybody okay?" Luno asked, peeling a slice of pepperoni off his forehead.

"As compared to *what?*" asked Clive.

Clive was okay.

"All that spinning made me hungry," said Chooch.

Chooch was okay, too.

"Hey, *look!*" Chooch shouted, pointing out the windshield.

In the distance, the swirl of mist that was once Freezorg was now settling. Then something amazing started to happen. The fog pulled together and transformed into a mass of water, which then crystallized into a swirling vortex of snow, then into a massive sphere of glistening ice.

Luno brought the pod to rest on the reformed planet and hopped down onto its snowy surface.

"Frosto?" Luno shouted, looking around. "*Guys?*"

Suddenly, the snow began to rumble and in moments, all four Freezorgs were surrounding Luno.

"What *happened*?" Frosto asked, scratching his frozen head.

The Freezorgs looked around and once they realized everything was okay, cheered! They picked up Luno, chanting "Lun-*o*! Lun-*o*! Lun-*o*!"

Luno was so happy, he didn't even mind when they accidentally dropped him.

"Well," Luno said to the Freezorgs awhile later as he stood on the wing of the delivery pod. "I guess this is good-bye—*again*."

Sheldon started to cry and hug Luno, which caused them to stick together again.

Once they pulled them apart, Luno climbed into the hatch after Clive and Chooch.

Frosto high-fived Luno, but missed and smacked him on the forehead. He then poured a handful of frozen coins into Luno's hands. It was enough for *five* pizzas! Luno couldn't believe his eyes.

He gratefully thanked them, waved good-bye, and slammed the hatch shut.

"Gee, Luno, that was real nice of you to help those guys," said Chooch, as Luno shifted the pod into gear.

"There is something I do not understand, Mr. Zorgoochi," said Clive, as they cruised along. "Why did you turn back to help them? You could have brought harm to yourself. It was not the *logical* thing to do."

"Sometimes the *right* thing isn't always the logical thing," said Luno, smiling, "but you do it anyway."

CHAPTER TWELVE

Home

As they zoomed through the quiet depths of space back to the pizzeria, Luno watched Clive contentedly pecking out his scientific findings on his little device and Chooch happily snoring away. Luno turned down Chooch's volume and concentrated on the drive back home.

VROOOOOM!

Suddenly, the pod was spinning, but Luno remained calm and simply pressed the stabilizer button. Everything was okay in a moment or two.

"Meteor?" Luno asked Clive.

"No, Mr. Zorgoochi," replied Clive. "It was another Quantum Pizza delivery ship."

RRRRRUUUUMMMMBBBLLLLE!

"*Now* what?" said Luno.

Emerging from the swirling cosmic mist before them was the biggest ship Luno had ever seen in his life. A steely black structure, the size of 100 spaceball fields, was moving slowly toward them. In letters along the side too large to be read from less than a hundred galactic miles away: QUANTUM PIZZA.

It was the mother ship.

As the enormous vessel moved closer, Luno could see little delivery ships buzzing out of the bottom of it, like angry hornets zooming out of an enormous nest, delivering pizzas all over the galaxy.

How can Zorgoochi Intergalactic Pizza compete with this? Luno thought as his tiny delivery pod floated past the massive Quantum Pizza ship, like a goldfish passing a whale.

Along the side in the center of the giant dot above the letter *i* was a porthole, and as Luno got close enough, he saw staring out of it a very angry—and ugly—face, its cyber-eye furiously swiveling about, which then came to rest on Luno. Somehow Luno just knew.

It was Vlactron.

Luno's spine froze as he and Vlactron locked into a stare while passing each other in slow motion. Luno

felt as if Vlactron were staring into his very soul. It was a moment he would remember for the rest of his life.

Suddenly laser fire violently rocked the little Zorgoochi delivery pod, breaking Luno's hypnotic stare.

He tried his best to not only avoid the fire, but to get them out of there as fast as possible.

Through the rearview screen he could see about a dozen Quantum delivery ships pouring out of the freighter. Luno didn't have time to be afraid. He slammed the pod into high gear.

"Hang on to something!" Luno shouted over the surging engine.

Chooch wrapped his big metal arms around Luno.

"Not *me*!" Luno shouted.

Chooch crawled under the control panel.

"What precisely do you suggest I hang on to, Mr. Zorgoochi?" asked Clive.

"Just *do* it!" Luno screamed and shoved his foot down as hard as he could onto the accelerator.

The fleet of ships surged ahead and, just as they were about to surround the delivery pod, pulled back and turned around, as if being recalled.

Regardless, Luno wasn't taking any chances and continued to pin the accelerator to the floor. By the time they passed through the Capellini Nebula and then entered the spiral arm of the Mezzaluna Galaxy, his foot was completely numb. He finally allowed himself to ease up and slow down once Industro12 was in view.

Luno drew a sigh of relief when he saw that the Zorgoochi Intergalactic Pizza sign was still there. He was determined never to let Quantum Pizza replace his family's business. He just had no idea how he was going to do it.

As Luno pushed open the front door to Zorgoochi Intergalactic Pizza, the familiar aroma of tomato sauce filled his nose and the heat from the pizza ovens warmed his bones. He was finally home.

"Son!" Geo said, arms open wide. "I'm so *proud* of you!"

"Here you go, Dad," Luno said, sliding his hand into his pocket.

When Luno pulled his hand out, it was dripping with water.

"Where's the money from the deliveries, Luno?" Geo asked.

Luno smacked himself on the forehead. He forgot to put the frozen money in the freezer in the pod. Now it was just a worthless puddle on the floor.

Luno was too afraid to look up. He saw his father's shoes move toward him. This was it. Luno was prepared for whatever came next. He deserved it. As Geo moved in closer, Luno screwed his eyes up tight.

I'mgonnadieI'mgonnadieI'mgonnadie.

"I know you did your best." Geo sighed, wrapping his big arms around Luno, pulling him close.

Then Geo showed Luno an order from the microscopic universe of Parva for 1,000 subatomic pizzas, 42 with extra electrons. It looked like Zorgoochi Intergalactic Pizza would be staying in business, at least for the time being.

Once Connie was done checking him for bruises, covering him with kisses, and crying tears of joy, Geo asked Luno how his deliveries went. Although he was bursting to tell them everything, Luno just shrugged.

"They were okay," Luno mumbled. "I guess."

Then Connie sat Luno down and plopped a huge plate of Plasma Parmigianino in front of him.

"*Mangia*," she said. "You look hungry. Eat."

The next thing he knew, he was waking up with his cheek resting on a nice, warm, but sticky pillow. Luno sat up and realized he had fallen asleep with his face in his plate. He peeled the mozzarella off his cheek and yawned, then climbed the stairs to his bedroom.

As Luno got to the landing, he saw the dark silhouette of Roog, waiting for him.

"Zo?" he asked. "How vas deliwery?"

Luno couldn't keep it to himself any longer. He told Roog everything—how the stories his father had told him were all true: the Mozzarella Monks, the Golden

Anchovy, Vlactron. *Everything.* He then told Roog that Quantum wasn't just trying to run Zorgoochi out of business, it was trying to run *all* pizzerias in the Mezzaluna Galaxy out of business in order to be the only one left.

"I know," Roog grunted. "Did you tell fazzer or mudder?"

"No, " said Luno. "I figured they have enough to deal with just trying to keep the pizzeria going."

"Goot." Roog seemed relieved.

"I don't know what to *do*, Roog," Luno confessed. "I mean, I know what I'm *supposed* to do, but I don't think I can."

"I vill help," said Roog, placing his metal claw on Luno's shoulder. "But parents muzt not know. Ho-kay?"

Luno agreed.

"Do you know vhy I train you hardest of all Zorgoochi?" Roog asked, looking Luno in the eye.

Luno shook his head.

"Because you are *zpecial*," said Roog, sounding more serious than Luno had ever heard him. "Vhen you ver leetle boy, I knew you ver de vun."

Luno's shoulders slumped with the gravity of the situation.

"Now ees up to you," said Roog. "*You* must find Golden Anchovy. Eet ees only vay to save Zorgoochi Intergalactic Pizza, Luno."

While Luno was slipping into his pajamas, Vlactron's evil face popped into his mind and a shiver went up his spine. He smoothed the hair sticking up on the back of his neck and looked out the window into the black expanse of space. Delivering pizza was dangerous business, but it was nothing compared to having to do battle with the biggest pizzeria in the universe.

Meanwhile, millions of galactic miles away, deep in the bowels of the Quantum Pizza mother ship, a scaly face with an angry, swiveling cyber-eye was watching a telescreen and on it was the grainy image of a pizza delivery boy looking out his bedroom window.

The face uttered just one word.

"Zorgoochi."

CHAPTER THIRTEEN

The Deepest Deep-Dish Pizza

Luno closed his eyes and leaned against the side of the greenhouse behind the pizzeria, hoping the sunlight would revive him after a night of wrestling with his pillow as he wrestled with the decision to keep everything from his dad and mom and take care of Quantum Pizza all on his own.

He blinked dumbly down at the glittering mosaic image imbedded in the cement of the greenhouse floor and the pattern the sunlight made shining through the complex latticework of its glass walls.

Luno heaved a sigh.

All he had to do was find the Golden Anchovy. How hard could *that* be?

Luno pictured himself as the Zorgoochi who took down Vlactron and smashed Quantum Pizza's grip on the galaxy. There would be holo-films about him, electro-stories written, monuments built, statues erected . . .

"Hey, *Luno*!" Geo shouted from the kitchen door. "*Andiamo!* Get in here! The lunch rush is starting!"

But first he'd have to make a lot of pizza.

There was already a steady trickle of humans, aliens, and robots from the nearby factories lining up for lunch and soon there would be a tidal wave of orders. Luno threw an apron on and grabbed some pizza dough.

"Dad?" Luno asked, attempting the Zorgoochi Pizza Toss. "Remember all those stories you told me when I was a kid that your dad told you about the Golden Anchovy?"

Geo grunted as he boxed up orders.

"Well, did Grandpa ever say where Solaro hid the Golden Anchovy?" Luno asked, trying to sound casual.

"We're *busy*, Luno," Geo snapped, absentmindedly snatching the dough away and effortlessly giving it the Zorgoochi Pizza Toss himself. "The story I told you about the Golden Anchovy was just that—a *story*."

"But, *Dad*—"

"*Look*, Luno, I used to tell you those stories to get you to go to sleep," Geo said with a sigh, nimbly pressing the dough to create the crust. "That was for *fun*, but now I need you to concentrate on *work*."

"Yeah, but does anybody actually know where it is?" Luno persisted.

"You have to put all that behind you, buddy," Geo said, ladling sauce on the dough. "And help me out *here and now*."

"One Cosmic Calamari Special!" Connie shouted, putting the ticket along with dozens of others on a revolving wheel powered by a machine invented by Luno's great-uncle Meccanico, which ran off the sonic vibrations of grumbling stomachs of hungry customers.

"*I'll* do it." Luno sighed, making his way to the seafood tank.

"Remember your seafood allergy, sweetie," Connie said, stacking steaming plates of food along her arm. "Wear the gloves."

"*Yes*, Mom."

"Because if you don't, you'll get itchy."

"*Yes*, Mom."

"And dizzy."

"*Yes*, Mom."

"And don't be a wise guy, mister."

"*Yes*, Mom."

Doing just as his dad taught him after many unsuccessful attempts and even more tentacle scars, Luno descended into the tank and knowing that calamari had no peripheral vision, stayed out of his prey's line of sight, then snuck up from behind and threw a net over it.

Once Luno wrangled the stubborn squid into a boiling pot, Roog had him peeling onions, an extra dangerous job due to the potentially lethal combination of an extremely sharp knife and blinding tears.

"Vhat deed I tell you?" Roog asked.

"Um, peel onions near a running tap?" sniffed Luno.

"And *vhy* do ve do dat?" asked Roog.

"*Because*," Luno droned, "the water draws away the sulfur and *that's* what makes you cry."

Luno followed advice he already knew and sure enough, *it worked.*

He then stepped up to the ticket wheel and grabbed another, intent on preparing a difficult order all by himself in an attempt to prove to his father he wasn't entirely incompetent.

"One deep-dish pizza," Luno mumbled.

He warily approached the proton collider with a glob of dough in hand. It was a standard collider, but jury-rigged for deep-dish pizzas by Luno's great-great-great-aunt Genia Zorgoochi and had been in the Zorgoochi family for years; like most of Luno's relatives, it was temperamental. Geo had shown him how to use it to make deep-dish pizza, but that was a *whole three weeks ago.* Luno knew how to switch it on, mostly because the word "ON" was printed right on the button. It was everything that came *after* it that was kind of fuzzy.

Luno dropped the dough in and started it up. The collider gave off a low hum, but that was about it. He peered down at the dough just sitting there. Then he noticed the knob, which determined the depth of the pizza, so thinking the deeper the better, Luno set it to *maximum*.

The collider hummed louder and the dough began to rotate, and soon it was spinning so fast, it was just a blur. When the machine began to shake and smoke billowed out of the sides, Luno began to think there was a slight possibility he may have ratcheted it a little too high.

Before he could hit the switch, a thin blue fog surrounded the collider, which soon enveloped Luno. He looked down and watched his feet lose contact with the floor. As he floated toward the ceiling, Luno attempted to swim back down to turn the collider off, but then something *else* happened.

He noticed through the fog that everyone and everything around him was moving in *reverse*: Dad walked backward, Roog pulled uncooked pizzas out of the oven, and Mom placed full plates of food back on the serving counter. Everything moved faster and faster. Soon Luno could see day and night flash by over and over again. After a while, things moved so fast, Luno couldn't focus any longer and blacked out.

"Vhat are you do-ink here, boy? You belonk *outside!*"

Luno blinked. He was sitting on the floor. He looked up and saw Roog standing over him. Luno couldn't quite place it, but somehow he looked *different.*

"Roog?" Luno asked as he got to his feet. "What just *happened*?"

"Dat ees *Meester* Roog!" Roog grunted, as he shoved a confused Luno out the back door with his metal claw.

Luno staggered around the garden, disoriented. Everything looked so *different*. There were no rows of herbs, tomatoes, or zucchini, no neat paths and no babbling brooks. Everything was overgrown and torn up.

And why were all those workers moving rocks, redirecting creeks, digging underground tunnels, and pouring cement where the greenhouse should've been? To make things weirder, Luno noticed beyond the fence that most of the surrounding factories and warehouses weren't there.

What was going *on*?

"Hey, kid!" an angry alien mason shouted. "Get offa my foundation!"

Luno looked down and saw he was standing in wet cement. He blinked dumbly at the alien holding an elaborate blueprint he was using to create the ornate mosaic in the cement with tiny colored stones. He felt someone yank him by his collar. It was Roog again and Luno realized what it was about him that looked different.

He looked *younger.*

Luno tried to find his father to explain just what was going on, but he was nowhere in sight.

"I find dees vun in kitchen," said Roog, dragging Luno across the rocks and debris up to a man working on the engine of a shiny robot.

"Hmmm?" The man closed the robot's back panel and stood up, wiping his hands on a rag. Luno noticed that the robot had a familiar deep dent on its panel before it perked up and spun around.

Roog gasped. "M-master?" he muttered.

"No, this is our new delivery autopilot," the man said, patting the robot on the shoulder. "Okay, William10, you're all fixed."

"Right-o, Boss!" the robot chirped. "Thanks!"

As Luno watched the robot happily clank away, he could've sworn it was the Zorgoochi's old delivery robot, but he was entirely too new—and too *nice*—to be him.

"Who do we have here?" the man asked, smiling warmly at Luno, then his expression changed to confusion. "Do I *know* you?"

"He is vun of de boys you hire to clear vacant lot," Roog said, still watching the robot. "And expand garden."

Luno couldn't understand why goose bumps crawled all over his arms as he and this man searched each other's eyes. Who *was* he?

Now *none* of this made any sense. Luno finally

figured out where he'd seen this face before. It was on every menu, every pizza box, and even on the sign on top of Zorgoochi Intergalactic Pizza.

It was Luno's great-great-great-great-great-grand-father, *Solaro Zorgoochi.*

But that was impossible.

Or *was* it?

The pizzeria looked bright and new, and William10 almost looked as if he just rolled off the factory assembly line, if that's who it was. And where did all the factories and warehouses go? *Or were they just not built yet?*

Luno's head spun with the unbelievable thought that he may have just traveled *back in time.*

"Mr. Zorgoochi?" someone shouted.

Both Luno and Solaro turned. Solaro waved, but Luno froze with fear.

It was a tall, lanky, bright green alien of the Reptilicon race, with a long tail and large feet. He may not have had a cyber-eye and was a bit awkward, but Luno knew.

It was *Vlactron.*

Luno reeled backward. Before he staggered into the glass wall of the greenhouse, Solaro pulled him back.

"*Easy* there, buddy," he said. "It's just my kitchen apprentice."

Apprentice?

Solaro told Luno that he never met someone as eager to learn about pizza as much as Vlactron. He explained that he had taken this bright young Reptilicon under his wing a few years ago and taught him everything he knew about pizza.

"We must talk, Mr. Zorgoochi," Vlactron said as he stomped up to them. His voice cracked a bit, trying to sound grave. "*Now.*"

"Later," Solaro said, putting an arm around a terrified Luno and walking away.

"It cannot wait," Vlactron replied, seething.

Solaro dismissed young Vlactron's impatience and continued on his way. As they passed what would someday be the greenhouse, Solaro proudly told Luno that not only did he design the mosaic on the floor and the intricate latticework himself, he planned out the entire garden, which would one day provide even more herbs and vegetables for his pizzeria. Luno could only nod, still trying to wrap his head around the fact that he was actually speaking to his great-great-great-great-great-grandfather and that Vlactron was his apprentice.

"You remind me of someone," Solaro said as they approached mounds of dirt and tray after tray of small containers of tiny sprouts. "So what was your name again?"

"Luno."

"Nice to meet you, Luno," Solaro smiled. Then he squinted at him and cocked his head. "I have a special job for you."

As Solaro handed him a tray, Luno inhaled the unmistakable aroma deeply.

"Erba Zorgoochus," Luno said, eyes closed.

"You know what that *is*?" Solaro gasped. "I cultivated that herb myself! How did you . . ."

"I've had *enough*!"

Luno and Solaro both turned to see Vlactron, throwing a tantrum, waving his arms, stomping his feet, and furiously whispering to Roog in the corner of the garden. Solaro noticed Luno's worried look and told him not to pay any attention. He explained that he'd been having problems with his apprentice, which has been the source of a recent argument.

Solaro gave him a map of the garden with specific instructions to plant the herbs according to a complex geometric maze-like path.

Luno diligently planted the sprouts following the explicit instructions. Later, while pressing through underbrush, Luno heard voices and quietly parted the bush to see who it was.

He held his breath as he watched Vlactron shouting at Solaro. The Reptilicon towered over Solaro, but Solaro seemed unfazed. Vlactron shouted about how Solaro was wasting his time expanding the garden and building a greenhouse, when he should be expanding his *business*.

"I've told you," Solaro said, "I need a bigger garden for my ingredients!"

"And I keep telling *you*," Vlactron argued, "it would be far cheaper to just use a synthetic substitute!"

"You mean *chemicals*?" Solaro asked, aghast.

"Those fools will never know the difference! Together we can create the biggest pizza chain in the galaxy!" Vlactron shouted. "Just give me the Golden Anchovy and I will show you!"

"I *knew* it! You didn't come here to learn about pizza," Solaro said. "You came here to get your hands on the Golden Anchovy!"

"No! I-I wanted to learn to make pizza f-from the master!" Vlactron said, trying to sound sincere. "And you said that maybe someday I would be your *partner*!"

"And once you got your hands on Zorgoochi Intergalactic Pizza and the Golden Anchovy," said Solaro, "you would conveniently dispose of me."

"That's not true!" Vlactron whined.

"I *trusted* you, Vlactron," Solaro sighed. "I taught you everything you know about pizza. We treated you like family."

"Without me, this pizzeria will never expand!" Vlactron snarled, his voice no longer awkward and youthful. "And never take over the universe!"

"I traveled the galaxy in order to spread peace, love, and pizza," Solaro said, not at all intimidated by Vlactron looming over him. "Not to take it over."

"You've wasted the Golden Anchovy's power!" Vlactron shouted. "It should be *mine*!"

"Well, I've hidden it! In fact"—Solaro smiled, tapping the side of his nose—"only a *Zorgoochi* will be able to find it!"

The argument escalated as Vlactron threatened to

open his own pizzeria, but Solaro refused to back down, which made Vlactron even *angrier*!

Suddenly a claw grabbed Luno's shoulder and pulled him to his feet. It was Roog.

"Get back to verk and don't eavesdrop, boy!" Roog grunted.

Luno went back to his planting, but noticed Roog stayed and listened.

Solaro walked across the open field with Vlactron following him. He spun Solaro around.

"Where *is* it?" Vlactron shouted in frustration, shaking him roughly. "I know you have it!"

Several human and alien workers rushed up and put themselves between Solaro and Vlactron. Undaunted, Vlactron furiously lunged at Solaro, but just in time, a pair of shiny red metal claws clamped down on Vlactron's shoulders, stopping him.

"*Nobody* touches the boss," said William10.

"I believe your apprenticeship is *over*, Vlactron," said Solaro. "William10, let him go."

The robot unclamped his claws and Vlactron straightened up and sniffed, trying to maintain his dignity. He spun on his heel and strutted away, but then stopped.

"I will destroy Zorgoochi Intergalactic Pizza, no matter how long it takes!" Vlactron shouted. "And someday the Golden Anchovy will belong to *me*!"

"It can't belong to anyone," Solaro calmly replied. "The Golden Anchovy belongs to the universe."

Vlactron stormed off. Solaro thanked his workers and patted William10 on the back, and then walked into the kitchen.

Luno just stood there, trying to absorb what had just happened and everything that *would* happen, if he didn't warn Solaro to stop Vlactron *now*.

As Luno ran to the kitchen, he tried to figure out a way to persuade Solaro to stop Vlactron without revealing that he was actually his time-traveling great-great-great-great-great-grandson from the future, because he knew he would quite possibly never believe him—

As Luno burst into the kitchen, he slammed into something. Just as he turned to see what it was, he was surrounded once again by a thin blue fog. He realized he had accidentally activated the deep-dish pizza proton collider. Luno floated off the floor and smacked himself on the forehead at his clumsiness, sending himself into a somersault.

He saw everyone and everything around him move forward faster and faster. Just as he was about to switch the collider off to tell Solaro to either stop Vlactron so he wouldn't become powerful in the future or at least tell him where he hid the Golden Anchovy, Luno stopped himself.

Transfixed, he watched Solaro working day after day, year after year, growing Zorgoochi Intergalactic Pizza into the finest pizzeria in the galaxy, and growing older. Then he saw generation after generation: Vulcanelli, Infinito, Tomino, Forza, Pomodoro, and finally his dad, Geo, each take over the business. Even in these brief flashes, Luno could see all the hard work, sacrifice, and determination each of his ancestors had to give to keep their little family pizzeria alive. He realized that they weren't just running a pizzeria, but keeping alive Solaro's dream of providing something good in the universe.

At this very moment, Luno knew he had to become worthy of the Zorgoochi name, maybe the most worthy of all. His ancestors' hard work would not have been in vain.

He would save Zorgoochi Intergalactic Pizza.

He just had no idea how.

"Where's my deep-dish pie?" Connie shouted.

The blue fog had lifted and Luno found himself being pushed aside by Geo with a glob of dough in his hand.

"Outta the way, Luno," Geo said. "I gotta make a—*hey!*"

Geo opened the proton collider and pulled out a perfect deep-dish pizza.

"Did *you* do this, Luno?" he asked, admiring the pizza.

Luno silently nodded.

"Nice job, buddy!" Geo shouted as Luno staggered out the back door.

Luno leaned against the side of the greenhouse and heaving deep breaths, tried to recover from his trip through time.

He looked at his watch. It was the exact moment he left.

Then he looked down and found himself standing in a very old pair of footprints he had never seen before in the cement.

And they were just his size.

CHAPTER FOURTEEN

The Pizza Pyramid

"Why didn't you just stop Vlactron back *then*?" Luno asked angrily.

"You dunt understand," Roog said, uncharacteristically sheepish. "I juzt *could not*."

"Tell your *dad*, Luno!" Chooch pleaded. "*He'll* know what to do!"

Roog nervously peeked around the corner of the greenhouse to make sure Luno's parents were still busy shutting the kitchen down for the night.

"For the hundredth time, Chooch," said Luno, "I have to do this without Mom's or Dad's help. They have enough to deal with just trying to keep the pizzeria going."

"Shouldn't you tell them about going back in time?" Chooch asked.

"Are you *kidding*?" Luno asked. "Mom was unhappy just letting me travel to another *planet*—what do you think she would do if she found out I traveled to another *time*?"

"But, Luno," said Chooch.

"Dad said Zorgoochi Intergalactic Pizza needed me to be grown up and responsible now," Luno said evenly. "I can't let him down."

"Luno ees right," said Roog. "He must prove to fazzer he can take over bizness."

"The intelligent approach would be to use the proton collider to return to the past," said Clive. "And stop Vlactron before he acquires power."

"Don't you think I already tried to go back again?" Luno snapped. "All I did was make a twelve-foot-deep pizza. I fell in and couldn't get out for an hour."

Luno racked his brain for a hint, a clue, *anything* as to where Solaro could've hidden the Golden Anchovy. It could be anywhere in the galaxy for all he knew: high on a mountain peak on a planet in the Nuga System? On an altar in an ancient temple on a planet in the Capellini Nebula? Floating somewhere in the Straciatella Quasar? Maybe buried somewhere on planet Earth? But, no, it was destroyed centuries ago.

As a wave of hopelessness washed over him, Luno

slid down the wall and sat on the ground with his head in his hands.

How can stupid little me defeat the biggest, most powerful alien in the galaxy?

Even with Chooch's kind words of encouragement, Clive's logical inquiries, and Roog's gruff coaxing, Luno still couldn't imagine where his great-great-great-great-great-grandfather had hidden the Golden Anchovy. Before he banged the back of his head against the greenhouse almost enough times to shatter the glass, he heard his father shout.

"Luno! Get me outta here!"

His father had found the deep-dish pizza.

Luno sighed, pulled himself to his feet, and trudged back to the kitchen.

After he helped his dad climb out, disposed of a hundred pounds of pizza, and finished mopping up, it was closing time.

Geo walked up to Luno and took the mop out of his hand.

"Listen, Luno," Geo said, giving Luno's shoulder a squeeze, "I know it must be kind of hard on you making deliveries all over the galaxy when you never even left the planet before and I just wanted to say thanks."

"But the deep-dish pizza . . ." Luno started.

"Ah, don't worry about that." Geo patted Luno. "I

once accidentally disintegrated my father and had to put him back together one molecule at a time."

Luno looked down at the floor, but Geo lifted Luno's chin with his calloused finger and looked him in the eye.

"I wanted to wait a few years," Geo said, "but it's time you joined."

"Joined *what*?" asked Luno.

His father looked around, then solemnly whispered, "The Pizza Pyramid."

Even though Luno had no idea what it was, he knew it had to be something important. He swallowed hard as his father led him into the walk-in freezer. They passed the frosty tubs of sauce, Pepperonisaurus tails hanging on hooks, and stacks of frozen pizzas. They came to the back wall and Geo pressed what Luno assumed, if he ever thought about them, were rivets.

A secret door popped open.

Luno cautiously stepped into a dark, cavernous room behind his father, who flipped on the lights. He gasped as a line of holo-portraits of the Zorgoochi ancestors flickered along the wall. The last was of his father, and beside it was room for a few more. There was even a small plaque, which read "Illuminato Salvatronic Zorgoochi," Luno's full name, all ready for *his* portrait when its time came. He had to read it a few times before it sunk in.

Fear and excitement pulled him across the red-and-white-tiled floor to a giant symbol of a slice of pizza with an eye in the center staring down at him, with the words PAX • AMORIS • PIZZA inscribed around it. The plaque hung on the wall over the far end of a long table with chairs around it.

Luno moved past a huge golden pizza cutter mounted on the wall engraved with the same pizza symbol with the eye in the center. There was also a rolling pin made from a Gragnick tusk engraved with a weird pattern, and a bunch of complicated cooking devices—all most likely created by his crazy genius ancestors.

There was a shelf crammed with trophies: the Galactic Pizza Award for the Hottest Pizza, But Not Too Hot It Burned the Roof of Your Mouth; Most Successful Deliveries to Hostile Solar Systems; Most Durable Box Under Zero-G Conditions; and Geo's seventh-grade Science Fair Award for a pneumatic olive pitter. Prominently displayed was Luno's Smelling Bee Award. He had always wondered what happened to it.

Luno read a framed news article about how Zorgoochi Intergalactic Pizza rescued a planet from starvation and one about Luno's great-great-great-uncle Tempo's mysterious disappearance. There were covers of various industry journals like *Plutonian Pizza Journal*, *Galactic Pizza Weekly*, and *The*

Interstellar Pizza Maker's News and Report, all with his esteemed ancestors on the covers. There was also a holo-photo of Luno's grandfather Pomodoro holding a pizza while shaking hands with the galaxy's first robot president, George Washingtron, and the vice president, John Quincy Android.

Luno's eyes were agog with commendations, ceremonial keys to planets, handwritten letters of gratitude, holo-photos of shrines, and statues of his ancestors.

Walking up from behind, Luno's father placed a hat on his son's head, which slid down over his eyes. Luno pushed it up and in the reflection of the glass cabinet he could see it was in the shape of a slice of pizza with the big eye in the center, just like the symbol hanging on the wall.

"This was your great-grandfather Forza's," Geo said, straightening it, then straightening his own. "So take good care of it."

Geo put an arm around Luno's shoulder and they proudly scanned the room together.

"Someday it'll be *your* turn to carry on Solaro's good work and look after Zorgoochi Intergalactic Pizza," said Luno's father. "That is, if it's still around."

He heaved a weary sigh. He sat Luno down and looked him in the eye.

"Now 'I don't want to upset you, son, but those stories I used to tell you when you were a little boy," he said evenly, "the Golden Anchovy, Vlactron, the *works*. Well, it's all *real*."

Luno didn't have the heart to tell his father he already knew. And, anyway, today was actually kind of a *slow* day. Considering he had been shot at, almost nibbled to death by tiny creatures, escaped being eaten by giant mushrooms, traveled through a wormhole, saved a planet, and went back in time, discovering the

far-out stories his father used to tell him were actually true was small potatoes by comparison.

"I know I told you when you got older that I made it all up, because your *mother* . . ."

There was a knock at the freezer's secret back door.

Geo rushed over and knocked a response. Then came another series of knocks. Satisfied, he opened the door and in streamed a group of men and women, all wearing the same pizza hats, followed by wide-eyed kids about Luno's age, also sporting the hats.

The adults reverently greeted Luno's father with "Pax, Amoris, Pizza," followed by a twisting wrist gesture, Luno figured represented tossing pizza dough.

"So *you're* Luno Zorgoochi," a chubby, curly haired boy said, approaching Luno, followed by the other kids, who all gathered around. "Thanks for leading us out of that cloudbank and back onto the spaceway. That was pretty brave."

The chubby boy introduced himself as Tony Galattico, heir to Proton Pizza in the Capellini Nebula. Then Luno met Concetta Cosmo, whose father owned Uncle Cosmo's, Frankie Boy Fazul Jr., whose parents owned Famous Fazul's, as well as several other successors to their family's pizzerias. He also met a somewhat dazed-looking girl named Zoola Zeta, whose parents owned di Mension Pizza and who appeared even more overwhelmed by the whole thing than Luno did.

Luno suddenly realized that they all thought of him as some kind of hero or the assumed leader of this group of the next generation of galactic pizza. Before Luno could set the record straight, the meeting was called to order.

The galactic pizza luminaries all took places around the long table with their children by their sides. Geo stood at the head and motioned for Luno to sit at his right.

Not only did he just find out about this secret pizza organization, but Luno realized his father was the *head* of it.

In unison, the adults launched into the Pizza Pyramid Pledge:

"We solemnly swear to make the best pizza, use only the freshest ingredients, and be a beacon of what is good and wholesome in the galaxy. Pax, Amoris, Pizza!"

After welcoming the Pyramid's newest members, Geo stood up and addressed the group.

"The reason for this emergency meeting is that the Mezzaluna Galaxy is heading toward a major pizza crisis of epic proportions!" Geo announced. "Not only is Vlactron attempting to destroy all of our pizzerias, but our esteemed member, Anthony Galattico, owner of Proton Pizza, has informed me that Vlactron is now trying to take control of all pizza ingredients, too! If he succeeds, the only pizza in the galaxy will be *Quantum*."

Mr. Galattico then stood and delivered a status report, declaring that most of the members of the Pizza Pyramid managed to safely elude Quantum's deadly delivery ships, however some weren't so lucky. He sadly listed the Pizza Pyramid's fallen members: Sal Zone of Stella Pizza and Calzones, Loo-E.G., the longtime autopilot delivery robot from Mama Andromeda's, and Phoebe Deimos from Apo Gino's.

"My son, Anthony Jr., tells me that Geo's son, Luno, heroically led several of the Pyramid's delivery ships to safety." Mr. Galattico smiled and patted Luno on the back, which was met with a round of applause.

"Why didn't you tell me about that?" Geo asked Luno, beaming with pride, but then his expression switched to concern. "Don't tell your mother."

"I—um," Luno muttered, his face bright red.

Mrs. Fazul stood up and said, "I know we all need to prepare our children to one day take over our pizzerias, but it's getting entirely too *dangerous*! I refuse to send my baby out there again!"

She sat down and sobbed. Mr. Fazul put his arm around her.

"Geo, my family's been a member of the Pizza Pyramid for generations," Mr. Fazul said. "Heck, my ancestors fought in the Great Pizza War, but enough is enough! I can't risk Frankie Boy's safety anymore."

"Fazul is *right!*" shouted Uncle Cosmo. "Quantum Pizza is killing my business and I don't wanna wait around for it to kill my *family*. We're shutting down our pizzeria!"

The meeting erupted into angry shouts and table pounding as Luno and the rest of the kids sat silently, eyes darting to one another. He noticed that Zoola Zeta seemed more concerned about keeping her Pizza Pyramid hat on straight than preventing Vlactron from destroying the last stronghold real pizza had in the galaxy.

Crash! Smash!

Wood, plaster, and support beams suddenly rained down as the ceiling gave way. Luno and a few of the kids scrambled under the table while the rest crowded the doorway back to the walk-in freezer.

"What's *happening*?" Concetta Cosmo shouted at Luno over the din, as the kids looked to him for an answer.

Luno gulped hard, then peeked up from under the table. He could see through the jagged hole in the ceiling straight up to the night sky where a Quantum ship was hovering. Its side doors opened and several ropes descended. Luno gasped as he watched what looked like large onion-shaped robots climb out and slide down the ropes.

"Take my hand!" Luno shouted over the chaos, reaching out to Zoola, who obediently grabbed hold and then took someone else's with her other hand.

Luno pulled the line of kids along, navigating his way through falling debris, screaming people, and a thick cloud of plaster dust. As he finally located the secret back door to the freezer, he heard the robo-onions touch down and then felt a sharp spray of liquid on the back of his neck with the unmistakable odor: onion juice! As he pushed the kids out the door to safety, his nose filled with the acrid odor, then his eyes burned and teared up uncontrollably.

Luno made sure every kid was safely out of the room and through the freezer, then pulled a few adults out as well.

He squinted through his tears and the cloud of dust for his father, but a robo-onion appeared wielding an onion juice blaster, pointing it right at him. As Luno fled out of the freezer, he turned and saw that the robot was following him, so he slammed the door behind him, but the robo-onion simply marched straight through it, followed by several more.

Luno ran to the back of the kitchen and found the kids recovering from the effects of the noxious liquid. A few were standing around Zoola, who was lying on the floor.

"I don't think she's breathing!" Frankie Boy shouted. "*Do* something, Luno!"

Before Luno could tell him he had absolutely no idea how he could possibly help, Tony pointed over Luno's shoulder and shouted, "Look!"

It was a robo-onion lifting an onion-juice blaster and marching straight for them! The kids hid behind Luno as he outstretched his arms to shield them.

This was it. Luno was going to get blasted at point-blank range and be permanently blinded or *worse*. As he backed up, Luno's hand touched the wall, but then touched something *else*. As the robo-onion took aim, Luno saw what it was and grabbed hold.

Just as the robo-onion squeezed the trigger, Luno slammed the fire-alarm handle down as hard as he could. Before the onion juice could hit them, water rained down everywhere, drenching everything in sight.

Now able to see, Luno looked down at Zoola. Her eyes flickered open. She saw Luno's face and smiled. In the midst of the chaos, Luno smiled back and helped her up.

"Um, thanks," Zoola said, "I . . ."

"Hey! My eyes don't hurt anymore!" shouted Tony, as they all pushed past the confused robot futilely firing its blaster.

The steady downpour from the sprinklers not only rendered the onion juice powerless, but the robo-onions, too. The robots wandered around, spraying everyone to no effect.

"How did you know to do that?" asked Frankie Boy.

"The water draws away the sulfur in the onion, " said Luno, "and that's what makes you cry."

"They *were* right, Luno," Zoola said dreamily. "You *are* pretty amazing!"

"I, um—" Luno mumbled.

"Luno!"

Luno turned to see his mother. Even though she was soaking wet, he could tell she was crying.

"Are you alright?" she asked, hugging him.

"Where's *Dad*?" Luno asked.

"I don't know," she shouted, searching the chaos. "We have to find him!"

Luno told his mother to stay put and ran back toward the freezer, but before he could, a dark towering figure swept through the broken door.

It was Vlactron.

Luno froze.

He was no longer the young, gangly Reptilicon from 200 years ago. Vlactron had grown into a dark formidable presence, with an aura of evil swirling around him.

Vlactron coolly scanned the kitchen and, seeing his robo-onions now useless, raised his clenched fist.

"Calamari!" he summoned. "Attack!"

Suddenly a troop of giant mutant squids slithered through the doorway behind him and wrapped their tentacles around some of the adult members of the Pizza Pyramid.

The kids threw pots, pans, and anything else they could get their hands on at the Calamari, but in return were doused with sticky black ink. Luno knew that even just a drop of that ink would cause him to not only blow up like a balloon but, as he was constantly reminded, to stop breathing.

"Dad!" Luno shouted as he spotted his father, bruised and hurt, limping toward him. But before Geo could reach Luno and his mother, a tentacle wrapped around his waist. Luno's mom lunged toward Geo to try to pull him free, but was knocked to the ground by another one of its tentacles.

As Luno helped her up, he saw the Calamari drag Geo, as well as the other Pyramid members, toward the freezer.

Remembering his kitchen training, Luno stayed out of the Calamari's direct line of sight and ran at it from behind with the first thing he could find, a giant frying pan. But before he could whack it on the head, another Calamari wrapped its tentacle around Luno's boot and lifted him into the air. As he hung upside down, Luno was sprayed with the black ink, then cast aside like a rag doll.

Now having captured all of the galaxy's master pizza chefs, Vlactron turned to the bruised and beaten crowd.

"Bid your good-byes to your loved ones," he snickered. "Because they will be working for *Quantum Pizza* from now on!"

Vlactron then ordered the robo-onions and Calamari back to the ship. He looked around the kitchen and spotted Luno, collapsed against a wall, wheezing, his allergies starting to kick in. Vlactron slowly walked over to Luno and then stood over him, looking down with a sinister grin, his cyber eye swiveling.

"If you ever want to see your father again, *you*, Illuminato Zorgoochi, and only you, must personally bring me the *Golden Anchovy!*"

Then Viactron marched away as the Calamari dragged Geo along with the rest through the secret doorway and onto the Quantum ship.

"Luno! Find the Golden Anchovy," Geo shouted. "But don't ever hand it over!"

Connie rushed over to Luno and took out an allergy pen. She pulled the cap off with her teeth and sunk the needle deep into his leg.

As his mother cradled him, Luno gasped for breath, helplessly watching his father being dragged away.

"Dad," Luno gasped. "I'm sorry."

CHAPTER FIFTEEN

The Golden Anchovy

Connie finally fell asleep.

Luno walked back down to the kitchen, through the walk-in freezer, and into the Pyramid Room, which wasn't a room as much as a pile of smoking debris with walls around it.

The first light of day poured through the hole in the ceiling as morning rose on Zorgoochi Intergalactic Pizza. Or at least what was left of it. The holo-portraits were destroyed, as well as a bunch of other irreplaceable family relics.

As the dust settled, he thought about the last ten hours: the Pizza Pyramid meeting; the attack from

Vlactron; Dad's kidnapping; then the long dark night with his mom crying, crying, crying.

But that didn't stop Luno from being *mad*.

"When I was little, Dad used to tell me about the Golden Anchovy, but when I got older, he told me it was all made up," Luno had said to his mom a few hours earlier. "If it was all *real*, then why did you make Dad tell me it *wasn't*?"

"Maybe because I didn't *want* it to be real," his mother sighed, brushing back a tear. "I guess I always thought I'd be able to protect you from it all. I wish I never allowed your father to persuade me to let you leave Industro12, but the pizzeria was in trouble and we really needed your help."

Mom explained to Luno that for years, she heard stories about the Zorgoochis, but always thought most of it was exaggerated ancient family history. It just *had* to be.

"Sometimes I wonder why I married into this crazy family in the first place," she said, shaking her head.

Connie found out the family stories, the Golden Anchovy, and Vlactron were all real the day Geo brought her into the secret meeting room behind the freezer.

"And that Pizza Pyramid with their silly hats and secret handshakes!" She rolled her eyes. "When they started it about two centuries ago, it was just a group of pizzeria owners helping one another with things like where to buy the best kitchen supplies or to let the others know which kinds of aliens ate pizza delivery boys. You know, typical business concerns," she said. "That is, until about seven or eight years ago, when Quantum Pizza started delivering just outside the spiral arm of the Mezzaluna Galaxy. *That's* when the trouble began."

And that's when Geo had brought her into the secret meeting room for the first time.

From that point on, the Pyramid meetings focused on the members banding together to protect one another from Quantum and keeping their pizzerias going.

His mother started to cry again and Luno wanted to cry, too, but knew it would just make things *worse*. As he kept handing her tissues, he tried not to think about maybe never seeing his father again and concentrated on getting him *back*.

"Mom?" Luno gently asked. "Do you have any idea where the Golden Anchovy *is*?"

"Where it *is*?" Connie snapped and, with an angry look, spat. "I didn't even think the thing was *real* until a few years ago!"

She sighed and looked at Luno with bloodshot eyes. That's when he took her by the arm and led her upstairs.

"Now I have to figure out how to save your father," Connie said, as the door to her bedroom hissed open. "And once I do, I'm gonna strangle him."

"Get some sleep, Mom," said Luno.

They hugged and her door hissed shut.

Luno now looked around the meeting room. Even though it was in shambles, it was the history of Zorgoochi Intergalactic Pizza. *His* history, and like Geo said, one day it would be his turn to look after the pizzeria and carry on Solaro's good work.

Then it hit him.

Today was that day.

Then something *else* hit him. It was a piece of the ceiling, so he decided to get out of there before the rest of it came down on his head. As Luno walked to the greenhouse, he thought about how every year, he and his family—aunts, uncles, cousins, and grandparents— all gathered to celebrate Solaro's birthday. It was his great-great-great-great-great-grandfather's one request, other than that it had to be celebrated right there in the greenhouse. Maybe he wanted to make sure his family got together at least once a year.

Luno's best memories were those parties. The one he remembered most was the year there was a thunderstorm. Little Luno watched the dark clouds roll in and the lightning flash through the greenhouse ceiling. Rain pelted the glass and thunder shook it, but he knew nothing would ever touch him and nothing bad would ever happen because he was surrounded by his family and they were safe inside Solaro's greenhouse.

Now Luno looked up at that glass roof hanging over

his head and noticed a small crack. He thought about how fragile it really was and how little it would take for it to shatter and the bad things in the galaxy to pour in and . . .

Rap-rap-rap.

Luno turned to see Chooch anxiously tapping on the window and Clive standing next to him tapping away at his device, so he got up and went outside.

"How are you gonna get Dad back, Luno?" Chooch asked anxiously.

"Taking into account Quantum's estimated weaponry, manpower, and sheer magnitude of operation, I have calculated the probability of you defeating Vlactron," said Clive.

"So what is it?" asked Luno.

"The odds against it are so staggeringly high," said Clive, "it would take me approximately four days to recite the number."

"That's just *great*," said Luno.

"I was under the impression you would be disappointed, Mr. Zorgoochi," said Clive.

"I *am*, you clueless bulb of garlic!" Luno sighed and rolled his eyes. "I was being *sarcastic!*"

"Please explain—"

"*Not* a good time, Clive," groaned Luno. "I still have to figure out if I should give the Golden Anchovy to Vlactron or not, that is if I can actually *find* it."

"But you said that Dad told you to never hand it over!" said Chooch.

Luno flopped to the ground.

"I don't know what to do!" he moaned. "I—"

"You already know vhat to do."

Luno looked up. It was Roog.

"Now *do* it. At least dat's vhat *fazzer* vould say," he said, helping Luno to his feet with his metal claw. "I tink he vould vant you to hand over Anchowy."

Even though it was against his father's wishes, Luno decided Roog was right. Geo may have told him not to hand it over, but it was probably because he didn't want anyone to get hurt. Now all Luno had to do was find something that his great-great-great-great-great-grandfather hid over 200 years ago that no one, including the most powerful alien in the galaxy, could get his claws on. Luno didn't bother asking Clive what the odds were of him locating it. He didn't want to know.

"Tink of vhere it could be," said Roog, tapping Luno's head sharply with his metal claw. "Tink! Tink!"

As Luno tinked until his brain hurt, a question suddenly popped into his head.

"How did Vlactron know about the secret meeting?" Luno wondered.

"Vhat ees dun, ees dun." Roog waved the question away. "You haff more impordant tings to tink about."

Then Roog told Luno that he worked him harder

than any of his other ancestors because he was *special*. He knew he would find the Golden Anchovy in order to save his father.

Luno wished he were as sure as Roog.

"Leave boy alone," Roog said, holding Clive and Chooch back as Luno wandered away into the garden, lost in thought.

"I wouldn't know where it was even if it was right under my nose," Luno sighed, sitting under an olive tree. He puzzled over what Solaro said to Vlactron as he tapped the side of his nose. *Only a* Zorgoochi *will be able to find it!*

What did *that* mean?

A soft breeze drifted through the garden and Luno inhaled deeply. It was as if his nose had pulled him to his feet and made him follow the aroma of Erba Zorgoochus, leading him down the complex pattern he himself planted years ago. He ambled along footpaths, under canopies of herbs, and over small wooden koi-pond bridges.

The trail came to an end at a little pool of water at the edge of the garden, one he had never taken much notice of before.

Luno sat cross-legged on the rough wooden bench no doubt made by Solaro, and stared into the water, watching the orange, copper, and red fish serenely swim about. They didn't worry about the future or even the past. They didn't know anything but *right now.*

Lucky.

He grew angry at the fish, but then was embarrassed for being angry at a bunch of fish.

Luno couldn't understand why he was just sitting there and not out looking for the Golden Anchovy or, at least, trying to figure out where it was. Geo and the rest of the Pyramid were Vlactron's slaves; it was only a matter of time until real pizza was obliterated from existence, and after 200 years, his family's pizzeria would be closed forever. And it would be all his fault.

Yet all he could do was watch the stupid fish.

Luno's eyes rolled upward and fluttered closed, as he still sat cross-legged on the bench, but he didn't fall asleep.

He felt like a cheese curd, blissfully bobbing in water. The universe was collapsing all around him and Luno wasn't afraid anymore. He was separating from the whey and floating upward.

Splish! Splash!

Luno opened his eyes. He had no idea how long he'd been sitting there. Were the suns rising or setting?

Splish! Splash!

Luno peered into the pond as if waiting for something to happen.

And after a few moments, it did.

A fish, smaller than the rest, timidly peeked out from

the shadow under the bridge. It cautiously swam toward Luno. He crouched down and saw it was glowing.

Even though he'd never seen the Golden Anchovy before, Luno had pictured it in his mind so clearly for so long; he felt less like he was seeing it for the first time and more like he was seeing it again after many years.

Sitting there, Luno didn't feel like he had just done what dozens of others for almost 200 years hadn't, because he didn't feel like he had really done anything at all. In order to find the Golden Anchovy, Luno always thought he'd have to fight bloodthirsty aliens, solve complex riddles, or travel to the far reaches of the galaxy. But he *hadn't.*

Roog always told Luno that he had Solaro's keen sense of smell. Maybe Solaro used Erba Zorgoochus to lead to the Golden Anchovy's hiding place knowing that one day he'd have a descendant who would inherit his super-sensitive nose. Maybe *that's* why he tapped the side of his nose when he told Vlactron 200 years ago that only a Zorgoochi would be able to find it. And maybe the garden, the greenhouse, and even the pizzeria are all an elaborate hiding place for the Golden Anchovy. Luno couldn't decide if his great-great-great-great-great-grandfather was a total genius or a total lunatic.

Luno had waited for this moment for such a long time and now it was here. Even when his father said the stories about the Golden Anchovy were just that, *stories*, a tiny piece of Luno never stopped believing they were real no matter how hard he tried.

Luno stepped into the pond and the tiny fish excitedly wriggled around his boots, as if asking to be picked up.

"I *told* you, you zilly robot"—Luno could hear Roog shouting in the distance—"leave boy *alone!*"

"Luno!" Chooch shouted, as he pushed his way through the bushes, followed by Roog and Clive. "*There you are!*"

Luno placed his finger to his lips to shush them and silently waved them over. He pointed down and was about to scoop up the Golden Anchovy, but remembered his allergies. As Chooch bent over to get a closer look, Luno popped Chooch's helmet off and placed it in the water. The Golden Anchovy swam right into it and Luno held it up high for everyone to see. The little fish circled the water, happily emitting a golden glow.

"You found it," Roog said, placing a claw on Luno's shoulder. "Right vhere Solaro left for Zorgoochi to find zum day. Hokay, lezz go."

"It is my understanding that if you touch the Golden Anchovy, you not only experience a vision of your heart's true desire, so to speak, but then are guided and protected by its power in order to achieve said desire,"

Clive said, as they made their way to the greenhouse.

Luno nodded.

"Well, then," said Clive, "is there some intelligent way for you to utilize its power in order to defeat Vlactron?"

"Hey *yeah!*" Chooch shouted, reaching for the Golden Anchovy. "You should hold it, Luno! Then—"

"No!" grunted Roog, slapping down Chooch's big metal hand. "Luno must give Anchovy to Wlactron to get fazzer back. Bezides, boy has zeefood allergy and if he touch, he *die!*"

"*Yeah*, but he could get an allergy shot right after he—" said Chooch, then suddenly powered off and stood there frozen.

"Oh, look at dat," said Roog, patting Chooch's back. "Zilly robot broken."

This never happened before and Luno was worried. Even though he was a giant pest, Luno wanted to fix Chooch right then and there, but Roog reminded him that they had to get the Golden Anchovy to Vlactron as soon as possible to save Geo.

"I believe I can repair Chooch," offered Clive. "He appears to be a standard commercial pizza oven model 32NWO with slight modifications."

"Zee?" said Roog, as he pushed Luno along. "Wegetable vill fix robot. Lezz go."

Roog pulled open the glass door and Luno walked into the greenhouse, sloshing the water and the Golden Anchovy around. They walked up to a table covered with dozens of empty tomato sauce jars, and Roog unscrewed a small one, then set it back down. He reached for the helmet but, for a microsecond, Luno hesitated.

"You no trust me, Luno?" Roog asked.

Luno handed it to him and apologized.

"Ees hokay," Roog said, pouring the water and the Golden Anchovy into the jar. "I dunt blame you. Eet ees most powerful ting in universe. I promise to be careful."

As Luno watched the little glowing fish swim around the jar, he realized that finding the Anchovy was easy compared to their next challenge: how to get around Mom.

They both knew about the iron will of Constellina Marie Zorgoochi firsthand and that she would never ever let her Luno set foot on the Quantum mother ship and hand the Golden Anchovy over to Vlactron, even to get Geo back.

Before Luno asked Roog if he could do it, Vlactron's words rang in his ears: *If you ever want to see your father again, you, Illuminato Zorgoochi, and only you, must personally bring me the Golden Anchovy!*

Clive and Chooch entered the greenhouse.

"After a thorough diagnostic scan," said Clive, "I

found nothing wrong with Chooch's system other than it was simply powered off."

"I must've bumped into a tree branch and it hit my power switch," Chooch said sheepishly. "I'm so *clumsy!*"

As he consolingly patted the robot on the back, Luno got an idea. He immediately got his toolbox and rushed to his room.

Luno emerged an hour later.

"Vee go *now?*" Roog anxiously asked Luno.

"Not yet," said Luno, handing Clive and Chooch a supply list. "There's no way my mom is going to let me go to the Quantum mother ship and hand over the Golden Anchovy to Vlactron."

"But Wlactron zaid it muzt be you who deliver it," said Roog. "You *muzt* go!"

"I *will* go," said Luno. "*And* stay home, too."

"The laws of physics do not allow for this to occur, Mr. Zorgoochi," said Clive.

"Yeah," said Chooch, "how can you be in two places at the same time?"

"Just go to the junkyard and get me everything on this list," said Luno as he handed them a piece of paper, "and I'll show you."

Clive, Chooch, and Roog spent the next few hours gathering scraps of metal, plastic, and titanium, and harvesting circuit boards, micro motors, and sub-atomic engines.

"Here," Roog said, wheeling a full wheelbarrow into Luno's room, which was now strewn with diagrams, lengths of tubing, and tiny gears. "Make it znappy! Vee haff to go zoon!"

For the next few hours, Roog nervously paced in front of Luno's bedroom door, listening to him welding, hammering, and screwing the pieces together.

Finally, the door hissed open and Luno peeked his head out. He looked tired, but happy.

"C'mon in," he said, as Clive, Chooch, and Roog walked past him.

"Sigh," said the tall, awkwardly assembled robot wearing Luno's old space suit.

The Luno Bot moped around Luno's room, kicked some dirty laundry, and then climbed into bed.

"Watch *this*," Luno said.

"Are you okay, sweetheart?" Luno asked, trying to sound like his mother.

"I'm *fine*, Mom," Luno Bot droned.

"Do you want something to eat?" Luno asked.

"Um, no thank you. I just want to sleep." Luno Bot sighed. "I love you."

"I'll just put him in my bed," Luno said, patting his

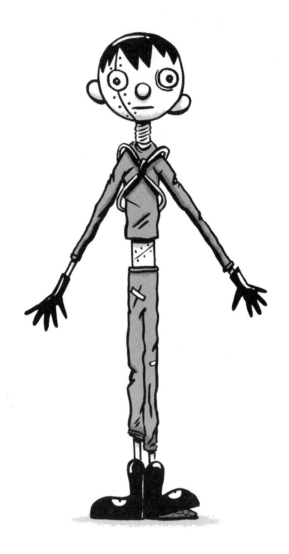

new creation. "And we'll be back before she even knows I was gone!"

Luno proudly looked to them for approval.

Clive had an alphabetical list of notes, suggestions, and improvements; Chooch asked if Luno Bot was his new brother; and Roog said it was *goot enough, zo lezz go!*

"Sure, Roog, go ahead," Connie sighed after Roog asked if he could take the delivery pod to stock up in case some customers showed up at lunchtime. Business had dropped off considerably ever since Vlactron kidnapped the Pizza Pyramid members. Since then, Connie Zorgoochi had been trying to come up with a plan to rescue her husband and keep the pizzeria going at the same time. There weren't many orders, so she didn't ask Luno to help her, assuming he was still recovering from his allergy attack and everything else that had happened.

"Tanks, Mrs. Z," grunted Roog, grabbing the keys. "You take care of yourself and dunt vorry about boy, heel be hokay. Just leave alone for now."

Roog climbed into the delivery pod, switched the engine on, and took off.

"Did you tell her not to bother me?" Luno asked, crawling out from underneath the control panel. "And let me sleep?"

Roog grunted.

Clive and Chooch climbed out of the onboard freezer.

"It's about *time!*" said Chooch, shivering. "I was starting to get a brain freeze in there!"

Luno took the pilot's seat.

The delivery pod burst through Industro12's

atmosphere, then entered the vast expanse of space. It was headed toward the Quantum mother ship, which was currently in the center of the Baccala Nebula.

The Golden Anchovy swam about in the little jar, its golden glow illuminating the dashboard where it sat. Luno watched it, transfixed, thinking about how it had helped Solaro bring peace, love, and pizza throughout the galaxy so many years ago. Luno still couldn't quite wrap his head around the fact that not only was it real, he was the one who found it.

But now he had to hand it over and not to just *anyone*, but to the most evil, vicious alien in the galaxy, who used to give him nightmares when he was growing up and was his family's pizza rival to boot!

But it would be worth it. He would save his father and bring him back home. Luno couldn't wait to see his face when he showed up.

But *then* what? Luno hadn't really thought about what would happen *after* he gave the most evil alien the most powerful pizza topping in the universe. Maybe his dad *was* right. Maybe he shouldn't hand over the Golden Anchovy. But, *no*, he had to save his father. He'd figure the rest out later.

"I-I couldn't have done it without you." Luno turned to Roog as he piloted the delivery pod. "Thanks and my family thanks you, too."

Luno's face suddenly became flushed and he

looked awkwardly down at the instrument panel. It just sort of came out. Even though he wished he could take it back, Luno still meant every word. Roog truly *was* part of his family.

"You're velcome, boy," Roog grunted.

"I may drop it or something," said Luno, handing the jar to Roog. "*You* take it."

"Quantum ships at 3:45!" Chooch shouted.

Luno was startled and almost dropped the jar, but Roog deftly snatched it before it was smashed to pieces.

"Hokay," Roog said, clutching the jar. "I hold for now."

Sure enough, Quantum ships were heading right toward them, dead ahead at twelve o'clock. Luno promised himself he would thoroughly explain the concept of time location to Chooch if they ever got out of this alive.

There were more ships than ever before and Luno truly had no idea how he was going to survive this one. Just when they were so close to delivering the Golden Anchovy and saving his father, Quantum was finally going to destroy them.

As the Quantum delivery ships surrounded the Zorgoochi delivery pod, Luno noticed something odd.

They weren't firing at him.

"Why aren't they attacking us?" Chooch asked, peeking out from under the control panel.

"Because I think they're *escorting* us," said Luno.

PART 3

CHAPTER SIXTEEN

In the Belly of the Quantum Mother Ship

Like a microscopic speck of flotsam drifting into an enormous space whale's mouth, the tiny Zorgoochi delivery pod flew into the yawning doors of the receiving bay of the colossal Quantum mother ship.

Luno's efforts to pilot were overridden by a tractor beam, which guided the pod toward the center of the bay. No longer having to steer, Luno and his crew gaped wide-eyed through the windshield at the interior of the mammoth freighter.

Thousands of delivery ships buzzed about in synchronized precision, all delivering pizza to the outer reaches of the galaxy. Luno looked up, but couldn't see an end to the rows and rows of windows, shipping bays, and who knew what else high above them. It seemed to go on forever. A network of glass tubes flowing with to-mato sauce and gleaming metal pipes pumping out chemical waste covered the walls like ivy, and in the distance, hundreds, or possibly thousands, of workers scurried about.

All of this just to make pizza, Luno thought.

Then he thought about his family's pizzeria and how there was just himself, his parents, and Roog, who did all the cooking, cleaning, delivering, and every-thing else to keep the pizzeria going. They had one kitchen and one delivery pod held together with parts from the washing machine, lots of glue, and a few prayers. It all seemed so broken-down, cobbled to-gether, and pathetically small. For the first time in his

life, Luno started to feel ashamed of Zorgoochi Intergalactic Pizza.

Clunk!

The delivery pod touched down.

As Luno made his way up the ladder, he felt Roog slip the jar into his pocket.

"Dunt forget dis."

Luno then climbed up, opened the hatch, and peeked out.

"Come out with your hands up!" the Quantum Guard general shouted. "The two of you!"

"Um, there's actually *four* of us," said Luno as he descended the side of the pod, followed by Roog, then Clive and Chooch.

They found themselves completely surrounded by a

dozen uniformed Reptilicon guards wearing helmets and boots, and carrying weapons that looked kind of like pizza cutters with very long handles.

"I'm Luno Zorgoochi and this is—" Luno started.

"We know who you two are," snarled the Quantum Guard general. "What are *they*?"

"This is Clive and this is Chooch," Luno said.

"I didn't ask you *who* are they," the Quantum Guard general barked. "I asked you *what* are they!"

"My *friends*?" Luno asked, terrified of giving a wrong answer.

Roog explained to the impatient general that Clive was essentially vegetable matter and Chooch was a robot, and that Luno had created them both.

The Quantum Guard general grunted, then explained that the mother ship's scanners only detected *sophisticated* life-forms like aliens and humans, not *lower* forms like vegetables and robots, which was why he thought there were just the two of them in the pod.

Even though scary-looking armed aliens surrounded him and the Quantum Guard general could no doubt snap his head off like twisting open a bottle, Luno had to stop himself from telling him off for calling his friends "lower life-forms."

"You two," the Quantum Guard general said, motioning to Luno and Roog with his weapon, "come with me."

"Yes, sir, General Zope!" replied the lieutenant general.

General Zope then told Lieutenant General Bomo to escort the vegetable and the robot to a holding facility. Hearing this, Chooch started bawling "*Noooo!*" and wrapped his arms around Luno, refusing to let go.

"It's *okay*, Chooch!" Luno shouted over Chooch's blubbering. "I won't be long. I *promise!*"

It took five guards to pry Luno loose and hold Chooch back, but he wouldn't stop crying. Then a guard jabbed Chooch with one of the pizza-cutter weapons, giving him an electric shock. Entirely rattled, Chooch began to fall apart.

As General Zope shoved Luno and Roog onto a hovering transport vehicle, Luno looked back and saw Clive helping Chooch put his pieces back together.

Chooch looked sadly at Luno and waved, then his hand fell off.

Luno drew a deep breath and focused on why he was here: *to get Dad back.* He placed his hand on his pocket just to make sure the jar was still there and breathed a small sigh of relief as he felt the Golden Anchovy swimming around.

As soon as they boarded the hovering transporter, Luno and Roog were whisked to the uppermost reaches of the ship. Level after level whizzed by, and soon, they were being pushed down a long dark corridor with a giant black door at the end, flanked by two very large and very mean-looking Mutant Calamari.

"We have the human Zorgoochi and his companion," General Zope announced and the Calamari mutely opened the door and stepped aside.

Luno was shoved in first, then Roog.

Luno found himself standing in the center of Vlactron's crimson lair. It was dark and dank and the stone walls seemed to sweat blood. Scattered about the room were skeletons and exoskeletons of various alien species mounted like trophies.

"Admiring my collection, Illuminato?" a soft voice asked.

Luno searched the dim room for the source and at the far end saw Vlactron seated on a high ornate throne tended to by several servants of some kind of insect species.

Luno slowly approached and Roog silently followed. As he drew closer, Luno could see that the throne was made of petrified limbs and appendages of different alien creatures.

"There is one from each and every race I've had to unavoidably eliminate." Vlactron gestured to the mounted skeletons. "They serve as a reminder to me that blood sometimes must be spilled in order to achieve great things. The greater the achievement, the more blood required."

Luno wanted to both collapse into a small heap on the floor and bolt for the door at the same time, yet he did neither. He just stood there, silent, standing his ground.

"You look familiar, but then again, all of you humans look alike to me," Vlactron said, examining Luno. "And although I've eliminated most of your kind throughout the Mezzaluna Galaxy, I don't have a *human* skeleton. You see, I haven't been able to eliminate them *all*, as evidenced by your presence here," Vlactron continued. "You humans are like insects. Even if you step on every one you see, there always seems to be *more*."

Vlactron then casually lifted his giant boot and, with one swift, violent move, brought it down on an unsuspecting servant, creating a sickening *crunch*.

Luno swallowed hard as the remains were quickly and quietly removed.

"Like these Anthropods, here," Vlactron said, gesturing to the scurrying insects. "There are entirely too many of them to exterminate, though I tried, so instead we've come to an agreement and now they work for me. However, you humans don't seem to be capable of seeing the wisdom of this arrangement, which leaves me little choice in what to do with you."

Luno gathered every ounce of courage and tried to sound brave, but his voice decided to crack at that very moment.

"I want my father."

"Oh, so you *do* speak," said Vlactron, grinning. "Well, we all want something, *don't* we, Illuminato? You want your father and I want the Golden Anchovy."

Vlactron stood up and Roog stepped back, but either out of courage or fear—he wasn't sure which—Luno didn't move a muscle. The insect servants scuttled into the shadows as their master slowly descended the throne, strode up to Luno, and towered over him.

"I was willing to wait over 200 years for the Golden Anchovy because I understood that above all, *patience* was what was required. You humans know nothing of patience with your short, pointless little lives. Reptilicons like me and this Crustacos here, we live much longer," Vlactron said, pointing at Roog.

Roog looked down.

"It's taken half my life span, but Quantum has gained almost total control over pizza in the Mezzaluna Galaxy," Vlactron continued. "And now with the Golden Anchovy, I will rule the universe!"

"Solaro used the Golden Anchovy to *help* the universe, not rule over it," Luno squeaked. "The Golden Anchovy is for *good*."

"A typical human sentiment!" Vlactron said as he sat down on his throne. "I've waited year after year for a Zorgoochi who would be able to find the Golden Anchovy for me and now here you are."

Even in the midst of the most terrifying moment of his life, a question couldn't help but pop into Luno's head and out his mouth.

"But how did you know I would be the one?"

Vlactron grinned deeply and gestured for Roog, who climbed up to the throne and stood at Vlactron's side.

"Why, my old friend Roog here told me." Vlactron smiled, placing a claw on Roog's shoulder. "He's been watching over you and your family for two centuries, waiting for an heir who would someday find the Golden Anchovy, and when he saw that you were capable, he informed *me*. Thank you, old friend, and thank *you*, Illuminato, for finding this treasure."

Luno felt as if he were falling. He couldn't breathe. He looked up at Roog, but Roog just looked away.

"Now, Illuminato Zorgoochi, give me what is rightfully mine," Vlactron commanded. "Give me the Golden Anchovy."

Luno's head spun as he unstuck his feet from the floor and forced himself to march to Vlactron's throne. He reached into his pocket and pulled out the jar. He couldn't bring himself to look at the Golden Anchovy.

"Bow," Vlactron whispered, licking his lips.

Luno clamped his eyes shut, bent his head, and handed the jar to Vlactron. Luno could hear an almost inaudible gasp as the alien took it and clutched it to his chest.

Then Luno straightened up and said, "Now for *your* part of the agreement, Vlactron! *I want my dad.*"

Vlactron looked straight into Luno's eyes and without expression shouted, "Calamari!"

Luno's stomach dropped.

The doors burst open and two large Mutant Calamari shuffled in and wrapped their tentacles around Luno's arms.

"Take him to the stockade with the others until further orders," Vlactron said, transfixed by the jar.

"But you zed vunce you get anchowy, you vould let dem go," Roog said to Vlactron.

"Well, I changed my mind," Vlactron replied. "You wouldn't happen to have *feelings* for those filthy creatures, would you, Roog?"

"Uff courz nut!" Roog sputtered, and shook his head.

As the Calamari led him out the door, Luno turned back to Roog, but he cast his eyes downward once more.

"If I decide to let you live, Illuminato," Vlactron called, not looking away from the Golden Anchovy, "perhaps we'll put that sensitive nose of yours into service for Quantum Pizza and use you as my personal food tester."

Vlactron was so transfixed by the small fish circling the jar, he hardly noticed the doors clanking shut. As he stared hypnotically at the fish lazily swimming in the jar in his hand, he revealed to Roog that he had an older brother named Rexrong whom he never knew since he went off to fight in the One Thousand Year Space War and was killed. Rexrong's personal belongings were shipped to his family and among them were several documents about the Golden Anchovy, something his brother appeared to be obsessed with.

"I spent my youth mostly alone on Reptilicus, finding solace in the legend and lore of the mythical Golden Anchovy," Vlactron said, almost as if talking to himself. "I read everything I could find about this divine creature, which gave power and guidance for one to achieve their truest desires, but when I learned it was real and that an undeserving human named Zorgoochi not only possessed it, but was wasting its powers, I knew it was destiny for it to be mine, so I apprenticed under him and spent years slowly building his trust only to be *denied*!"

"I know, Rex Wlactron," Roog grunted.

"So I left to build my *own* empire," Vlactron said, still staring at the tiny fish. "My rise to power was steady and strong, as if the hand of the universe cleared a path for my success. It was almost *too* easy."

He then stood up and examined the Golden Anchovy in a dim shaft of light.

"But by then, the Golden Anchovy's hiding place was lost to time, so I waited for the Zorgoochi heir to find it for me," Vlactron said, turning the jar in the light. "Within that time, I transformed myself from an undisciplined youth to a confident and determined adult with the biggest, most-powerful pizzeria chain in the Mezzaluna Galaxy."

Vlactron removed his glove, grasped the lid of the jar, and began unscrewing it.

"And now I will show the universe the Golden Anchovy's true strength with *my* grand vision!" bellowed Vlactron. "Upon my touch, the Golden Anchovy will be my guide and protector in fulfilling my life's purpose: *total galactic domination of pizza*."

But before he lifted the lid, Roog put out a claw to stop him.

"But, Rex Wlactron, you haff destroyed almost all udder pizzeria, and now dat Zorgoochis haff been ruined, the rest vill follow," Roog said. "Even *vithout* using Golden Anchowy, you are now undisputed pizza master of Mezzaluna Galaxy."

"Go on," Vlactron said, leaning back.

"As long as you possess it, there vill be no vun more poverful den you and now dat you haff Golden

Anchowy, no vun else can have it," Roog explained. "You haff taught me wirture uff *patience*, Rex Wlactron, zo perhaps vait until day vhen eet ees *truly* needed."

Vlactron considered Roog's suggestion as he screwed the lid back on.

"Zorgoochis are poverless now, Rex Wlactron," said Roog. "Let dem go."

Vlactron looked into Roog's eyes and without expression shouted, "Calamari!"

The doors burst open and two large Mutant Calamari shuffled in and wrapped their tentacles around Roog.

"Vhat are you do-ink?" Roog growled. "I haff been loyal servant for *two century*!"

"Yes, and you've served me well, but now your function is complete," said Vlactron. "And although you may have developed human-like emotions for those creatures, what is more disturbing is my suspicion of your allegiance."

"But I deliwer Golden Anchowy!" Roog shouted.

Vlactron gently smiled down at Roog as he struggled against the iron grip of the Mutant Calamari. As strong as he was, he couldn't break free.

"You, my old friend, are the very last one alive in the universe who actually knows that I apprenticed under Solaro Zorgoochi," Vlactron explained. "And once you've been disposed of, as well as the human race, there will be no one left to dispute that I was the sole inventor of pizza and not some lowly human."

"But I vill tell *no vun!*" Roog said, but Vlactron was unmoved.

"Take him to the stockade," Vlactron said. "And tell our head chef that for tomorrow's dinner I'd like a delicious broiled Crustaco with a side of drawn butter. But he must be sure to remove the metal claw first."

The Calamari dragged a kicking and screaming Roog away. The doors slammed shut.

"Hello, Uncle," a voice called from across the room.

Vlactron turned to see a small adolescent female Reptilicon walking toward him.

"Oh, hello, Elvina," Vlactron grumbled and turned his back to her.

Elvina marched up to the throne, snatched the jar out of Vlactron's hand, and examined it closely.

"What's *this*?" she asked, squinting into the jar.

Vlactron seethed with anger, but drew a deep breath and gently took the jar back.

"It is the Golden Anchovy," said Vlactron. "The most powerful pizza topping in the universe."

"Well, it doesn't *look* very golden." She looked at it again, tapping the jar. "Where did you get it?"

Vlactron explained that it was given to him as a gift from a boy named Luno Zorgoochi, who greatly admired and respected him.

"You should follow his example," Vlactron growled.

"And I'm sure he gave it to you *willingly*," she said sarcastically. "And that you didn't torture him or murder his family to get it."

"I have exterminated entire species for less insolence!" Vlactron shouted into Elvina's face. "May I remind you that you suddenly appeared at my doorstep with nowhere else to go, years after my brother was killed, and I took you in out of obligation to my family! I raised you as my own and for that you should be *grateful* and show me *respect!*"

"I HATE you!" Elvina screamed back at him and stormed out of the room, slamming the door shut, with a noise that echoed throughout the corridors.

Luno hardly noticed the echo of a far-off door slam as he was pushed onto the hovering transporter by the Mutant Calamari.

The way down was a lot quicker than the way up, and within moments, he was shoved off the transporter and led through the lower decks of the Quantum mother ship, past rows and rows of barred cells. They stopped at one and the doors automatically opened. He was pushed in. The bars clanked shut.

"Can we go home now, Luno?" asked Chooch.

"I agree with Chooch, Mr. Zorgoochi," said Clive. "I believe I have gathered enough data and I am ready to leave."

Luno ran over and hugged Clive and Chooch as hard as he could. He was never happier to see anyone more in his life, even if it was a super-intelligent gamma-ray-infused mutant bulb of garlic and a 32-galactic-ton whiney pizza oven.

Luno explained what happened, but more importantly, about Roog.

"Not only did I just hand over the most powerful pizza topping in the universe to the most evil alien in the galaxy, but I didn't even save Dad," Luno sighed. "And to top it all off, I got us thrown in here. I'm so *stupid!*"

"It's okay, Luno," said Chooch. "It's all water under the fridge. *We* still love you!"

Once again, Chooch locked Luno and Clive in a bone-crushing group hug.

"Break it up, you guys!" a guard snarled as he slid a pizza under the bars. "Here's your dinner: one large Quantum pizza!"

Luno squirmed out of Chooch's embrace and angrily grabbed the pizza.

"You know where this belongs?" Luno shouted as he yanked open a small door on the wall and shoved the pizza into it. "In the *incinerator*!"

"Suit yourself," said the guard as he shook his head and walked away.

"It is not an incinerator, Mr. Zorgoochi," said Clive.

"Huh?" Luno asked, furiously pacing the room.

"It is not an incinerator," said Clive. "It is a *trash chute*."

Clive then explained that as he and Chooch were being led to the cell, he gathered fascinating data about the inner workings of Quantum's mother ship from Lieutenant General Bomo, who also informed him that the trash was not incinerated, but loaded onto an auto-piloted garbage barge and then dumped in a far-off solar system. Luno rolled his eyes.

"*Not* a good time for a . . . ," Luno said, but then was

struck with an idea. He opened the trash chute and tried to climb in.

"Don't leave me, Luno!" Chooch cried, grabbing Luno.

"Let *go*, Chooch!" Luno's voice echoed. "I'm going to sneak off the ship through the trash chute and . . ."

Chooch pulled Luno's feet and they fell to the floor with a thud.

Clive reminded Luno that when they first got out of the pod, Lieutenant General Bomo told them that the ship's scanners detected sophisticated life-forms like aliens and humans. If he tried to escape he would be spotted immediately.

"Well, that's *it* then," said Luno, dropping himself onto the cot. "I didn't save Dad, Roog betrayed my family, Vlactron will rule the galaxy, and Zorgoochi Intergalactic Pizza will be finished forever."

Luno curled himself up into a ball. After a few moments, Clive and Chooch could see that he was crying.

"Hmmm," said Clive. "It appears, Mr. Zorgoochi, that you have sprung a leak."

Clunk!

Just when things couldn't get worse, Chooch began to fall apart.

CHAPTER SEVENTEEN

Through the Trash Chute

"Get *out!*" Elvina burst into the Quantum mother ship's security surveillance center and shouted at the guards, who were well accustomed to her emotional tirades. It was her favorite place to be because she was able to see everything that went on all over the ship and could control practically everything.

"*Beat* it!" she shrieked. "*All* of you!"

"But, Miss Elvina," Lieutenant General Bomo braved, "we're not allowed to leave our posts!"

The guards scrambled out of the room, but Lieutenant General Bomo stayed, gripping the arms of his chair as if to stop himself from bolting out the door with the rest.

"Do you want me to tell my uncle I caught you sleeping instead of monitoring the prisoners?" she snarled.

Terrified, he got up and headed out the door.

"Wait a minute," she said, pointing to a monitor. "Who are *they*?"

"New prisoners," he replied. "There's been talk around the ship that the human Zorgoochi handed over the Golden Anchovy to Rex Vlactron."

Elvina looked back at the screen and watched the boy weeping on his cot as a big goofy-looking robot kept falling apart and a vegetable creature put its pieces back together. She zoomed the camera in close on the human as he wiped the tears from his eyes. Elvina gently touched the screen with her fingertips, but then spun around to see Lieutenant General Bomo still standing in the doorway.

"I said get *out*!" Elvina screamed, throwing a radio communicator at him, but he closed the door before it could hit him and it struck the door with a *clunk*.

She turned back and gazed at the screen.

Through tearful eyes, Luno watched Clive snapping Chooch's pieces back into place, but then suddenly bolted upright and leapt off the cot.

"Hey!" Chooch shouted. "What're you *doing*, Luno?"

Luno didn't answer as he frantically pulled, yanked,

and unscrewed the parts of Chooch that Clive had just put back on. Within moments, bits and pieces of Chooch were all over the cell floor.

"You guys are lower *life-forms*!" Luno said as he opened the door to the trash chute and dumped Chooch's legs in.

"What do you *mean*?" Chooch wailed, but couldn't cry because his head was no longer connected to his fuel line. "Why are you throwing me away, Luno?"

"Please explain your actions, Mr. Zorgoochi," said Clive, watching Luno pick Chooch's head up off the floor.

"Don't you *get* it?" Luno asked as he thrust Chooch's head into Clive's hands and then continued throwing parts down the chute. "You guys won't be detected by the scanners!"

"Find a way back to the pizzeria and tell Mom to send help!" Luno told Clive and Chooch's head. "You two are our last chance to stop Vlactron before he takes over the universe!"

"Please furnish me with detailed step-by-step instructions as well as any diagrams and schematics that will be required to accomplish this task," said Clive.

"Yeah!" Chooch's head shouted. "We don't know what to *do*!"

Luno pulled the chute door open. "You're just going

to have to figure it out," he said, pushing Clive in. "Once you get to wherever the trash chute ends, reassemble Chooch, make your way back to the pizzeria, *and tell Mom to send help!*"

"But I don't *wanna* go, Luno!" Chooch cried. "I'm *scared!*"

"Remember"—Luno's voice echoed as Clive and Chooch's head slid through the trash chute—"send help!"

It took several painful minutes for Clive and Chooch to make their way through the complex intestinal network down to the trash sector deep in the ship's bowels.

Thunk!

Clive accidentally dropped Chooch's head as he landed on a massive pile of discarded boxes, pizza

crusts, and the remains of disobedient servants. It rolled and struck one of Chooch's feet.

"Ouch!" he shouted.

Clive picked it up, located Chooch's pizza oven torso, and reattached his head.

"Hey!" Chooch said, looking down. "You put my head on *backward*!"

"Actually, your head is attached correctly, Chooch," said Clive. "It is your *body* that is backward."

For the next few minutes, Clive scurried around, gathering Chooch's components and putting him back together.

"It's about *time*, Clive!" Chooch said, bending his reattached legs and straightening his head. "Luno said we're supposed to find a way back home and tell Mom to send help!"

"We must first locate an exit from this trash sector before we acquire transportation to Industro12," Clive said, switching on his device and scanning the trash hangar.

"Fascinating," Clive said, squinting at the screen.

"Didja find a way out of here?" Chooch asked anxiously.

"According to my ultrasonic scan of the ship, there is an elevator to the upper levels directly over there," said Clive, pointing to a door. "However, the complex plumbing system of this ship is far more intriguing and bears closer study, so I would like to further analyze its . . ."

Clive didn't finish what he was saying because Chooch was dragging him toward the door.

"It appears to be locked," said Clive, trying the knob. "This will allow me time to analyze the plumbing system, but only once I calculate how long it will take before we expire from lack of sustenance."

"You mean *die*?" screamed Chooch. "I don't wanna *die*!"

Chooch frantically pounded on the door, which quickly flew off its hinges and fell to the floor in a crumpled heap.

"Oops," Chooch squeaked.

They stepped over the twisted metal and headed down several dark corridors until they came to a freight elevator. They stepped in and the doors clanked shut. Clive instructed Chooch which button to press and they slowly ascended. The elevator shuddered to a stop, the doors screeched open, and they stepped out.

"Uh-oh," said Chooch.

"Fascinating," said Clive as he waved his device in front of him.

"DROP YOUR WEAPON AND PUT YOUR HANDS UP!"

They were surrounded by at least a hundred Arthropods wielding mops, brooms, and other cleaning tools.

"I said drop your weapon!" an Arthropod shouted, approaching Clive and Chooch, brandishing a broom.

"I think he's talking about your thingie," Chooch whispered, pointing to the device in Clive's hand.

"This is not a weapon," Clive explained. "It is a multi-phase subatomic analytical device, which stores and evaluates . . ."

The Arthropod snatched the device out of Clive's hand and examined it suspiciously.

"We don't wanna hurt anybody," Chooch pleaded, holding his hands above his head. "We just wanna go *home!*"

"I'm afraid we must turn you over to Rex Vlactron," the Arthropod said grimly, handing Clive back his device.

"But *why*?" Chooch asked.

"Because," said the Arthropod, "we are his slaves and must do his bidding."

"Please define the word 'slave,'" said Clive.

The Arthropod explained that, many years ago,

Vlactron came to Planet Cimex, their home planet, bearing gifts of Quantum Pizza, promotional buttons and hats, and coupons for free pizza, but it didn't take long for them to discover that Vlactron was less interested in being friendly and more interested in the Pepperonisaurus that roamed free on their planet.

Vlactron was invited as an honored guest to the Arthropods annual De-Tailing Celebration where they performed an elaborate ritual of painlessly removing the Pepperonisaurus's edible tails, which eventually grew back, providing the Arthropods with plenty of food for the entire year.

Vlactron instead wanted to slaughter the Pepperonisauruses, remove their tails, and cast the rest aside, even though they explained that it would eventually drive the Pepperonisaurus to extinction, then ultimately the Arthropods. When they attempted to stop him, Vlactron and his troops led a full-scale attack, killing many Arthropods.

"I made the decision to surrender in order to stop the slaughter of my fellow Arthropods, and in return, Vlactron allowed us to live and serve him. I am Xoboz, their leader, or at least I used to be," he said gravely. "So do you understand what a slave is *now*?"

As the Arthropods closed in on them, Chooch asked, "But don't you want to go back home?"

The insects looked to one another and bleakly

muttered in agreement. When Chooch explained to Xoboz that they were trying to save Luno Zorgoochi, a hush fell over the crowd.

"Is he a descendant of the legendary human pizza chef Solaro Zorgoochi?" Xoboz asked.

"Why, yes, he is," Clive replied.

The Arthropods excitedly muttered to one another.

"We have all heard of that most honorable human Solaro Zorgoochi," Xoboz said, immediately straightening up and slamming the floor with his broom. "It would be our honor to be of service to his kin."

Chooch explained that if they helped him and Clive get back to the pizzeria, they would return with forces to defeat Vlactron and his troops.

"And then you guys can go home!" said Chooch.

The Arthropods cheered!

"What's going on down there?"

Everyone scrambled about at the guard's approaching boot steps. Xoboz quickly instructed one of his workers to hide their new friends, and Clive and Chooch were hustled away.

"Get *in*!" an Arthropod whispered, as he opened the top of a dirty dumpster. "*Hurry!*"

"Ewww!" said Chooch.

"I do not understand. This receptacle is designated for trash," said Clive, pointing at the lettering on the side of the bin. "And I am not trash."

The Arthropod ignored their protests and shoved them in, then told them to keep quiet.

Clive and Chooch heard the sharp footsteps of a guard grow closer, stop right outside the dumpster, and then a muffled conversation. Chooch held his breath as the guard drummed his fingers on the lid and gasped when he heard him shout, followed by Xoboz's indecipherable reply.

The muted voices erupted into an argument and the guard pounded the top of the dumpster to punctuate his point. Chooch shivered with terror and held on to Clive, which made Clive's glasses fall off with a clunk.

The voices stopped. Chooch tried to make himself as small as possible, which wasn't easy.

"Did I hear something coming from inside here?" the guard asked, as the lid creaked open slightly.

"Most likely, sir," Xoboz said. "We've had a major pest problem, but I believe we have it under control."

The lid lifted a bit more.

"I wouldn't do that, sir," said Xoboz. "One of my workers was attacked by a pack of raveenos that live in the trash sector and was entirely consumed in ten seconds."

The lid slammed shut.

There was more muffled conversation, then footsteps, then nothing.

Chooch didn't move. The lid squeaked open again and the light flooding in blinded him and Clive.

"Get out!"

They looked up and saw that it was Xoboz, who then assured them. "It's all clear."

Chooch let go of Clive and they climbed out of the dumpster.

"There's only one way off the ship without being detected," Xoboz said, leading Clive and Chooch down a narrow hallway and up a flight of rickety stairs.

The narrow stairway opened up to an impossibly huge loading dock, the size of five spaceball fields, with a colossal trash barge docked in its port, just as Lieutenant General Bomo told Clive. They walked past dozens of Arthropods scurrying about, supervising the loading of the trash into the hold.

"The barge will be autopiloted to the Nuga System, where its contents will be released into space, and then it will return to the Quantum mother ship," said Xoboz, as he led Clive and Chooch up the steps of the barge.

"But we wish to go to Industro12 in the spiral arm of the Mezzaluna Galaxy," said Clive. "The barge's trajectory must be altered."

Xoboz explained to Clive that the ship's course was preprogrammed, unless overridden by someone in the control center on the mother ship, which was well guarded.

They entered a small room.

"The only other way to change the course of the barge would be to reprogram the autopilot inside *this*," Xoboz said, pointing to a large titanium-encased box. "But it is impossible to open it."

Fortunately, Chooch didn't know the meaning of the word "impossible," along with a lot of other words, so before Xoboz could tell them they would have to find another way, Chooch was yanking the 1,000 galactic-pound, 10-inch-thick titanium box off the floor. After a few seconds, the thick arm-size rivets attaching the unit began to creak and loosen, then ricochet around the room.

Within minutes, Clive disabled the autopilot's receiver and was reprogramming the barge's flight plan to Industro12.

"We may leave now," Clive said to Chooch, as he punched in the last few coordinates.

"Zorgoochi Intergalactic Pizza, here we come!" Chooch gleefully shouted, hopping up and down.

"Good luck," said Xoboz, shaking Clive's and Chooch's hands. "It has been a privilege to be of service to two brave and noble warriors in the fight against the oppression of a barbaric tyrant in order to bring about peace and freedom throughout the galaxy!"

"Let's *go*!" said Chooch.

"Please define the word 'luck,'" said Clive.

The grainy image of the trash barge leaving the dock flickered on a monitor in the Quantum mother ship's surveillance center.

A red light illuminated on the control board, indicating that communication with a service vehicle had been terminated and that it was leaving without proper clearance. Elvina quickly switched it off before the alarm sounded. She smiled as the barge slowly moved out into space.

As she ignored Lieutenant General Bomo pounding on the door, asking her to open it, Elvina turned to another monitor and watched the human boy nervously pace his cell and placed her hand on the screen.

"Zorgoochi."

CHAPTER EIGHTEEN

Back to the Mother Ship

"What have you two idiots done with my baby?!" Connie Zorgoochi shrieked, springing out of her chair as Clive and Chooch entered the pizzeria kitchen. She furiously pounded on Chooch's chest and shook Clive, making his glasses fall off.

"Where's my *Luno*?" she shouted. "And don't try to tell me *that's* him!"

She angrily kicked the Luno Bot crumpled in the corner.

"I'm *fine*, Mom," Luno Bot droned. "Um, no thank you. I just want to sleep. I love you."

Exhausted from sleepless nights of worry, Connie collapsed back into her seat. She wearily explained that after a few days of Luno refusing food, she decided enough was enough and brought him his favorite meal, her special eggplant Parmesan.

"And when he refused *that*, it didn't take me long to figure out he was a robot, so if you two don't tell me where my boy is, I'm going to turn *you* into a garbage disposal"—then she turned to Clive—"and chop *you* up and put you in a pot of sauce! *Now where's my son?*"

"You look like you could use a hug," Chooch said, smiling, arms open wide.

"Tell me where my son is," growled Connie. "*Now.*"

Chooch immediately hid behind Clive, who delivered a thoroughly informative account of everything that had transpired since Luno left the pizzeria several days ago. He was sure not to leave out the multitude of technical details of the Quantum mother ship, the velocity at which they traveled, and the more interesting aspects of the plumbing system. He could not comprehend why Connie didn't share his fascination with these riveting details and was more interested in Luno, who was far less intriguing from a scientific standpoint.

Chooch fearfully clutched the Luno Bot to his chest as Connie sat in stony silence with her head in her hands. After a few moments, she drew a deep breath, steeled herself, and stood up.

"Geo told me this day would come, but I never

believed him," she said, making her way to the walk-in freezer. "Come on, you two. We have a galaxy to save."

Clive and Chooch followed Connie over the debris, through the freezer, and into the Pyramid Room. They stood by watching her search the crumbling walls, shaking her head and muttering to herself.

Her eyes rested on a golden pizza cutter mounted on a wall and she climbed over a fallen ceiling beam to get to it. She squinted at the words engraved on the circular blade and turned it like a dial from *mild* to *medium* to *spicy* to *extra spicy* and then finally to *super hot*.

"Why did I marry into this crazy family?" She sighed, shaking her head. She pulled down hard on the handle, which immediately caused a low decibel hum to pulsate throughout the room.

"Look," she said, pointing up through the giant hole in the ceiling to the roof of the pizzeria.

The large coiled antenna perched on the very top of Zorgoochi Intergalactic Pizza glowed in time to the throbbing hum. Connie explained to Clive and Chooch that right at this very moment, a secret sub-radar signal invented by great-great-great-aunt Genia Zorgoochi, was being beamed to antennas atop the other Pizza Pyramid pizzerias throughout the spiral arm of the Mezzaluna Galaxy. The pizzerias were now officially on Super Spicy Alert for the first time since the dark days of the Great Pizza War of Deep Dish vs. Thin Crust.

The signal was used to announce the current state of pizza in the galaxy, as well as summon the Pizza Pyramid members, but being that all of them were now slaving away in the Quantum kitchens, it was the members' spouses and children, the junior members, who answered the call and who were assembled on the roof of the pizzeria a few hours later.

"I can't believe they actually captured *him!*" said Tony Galattico as he and several of the Junior Pyramid members boarded the massive trash barge hovering over the pizzeria.

"Yeah!" Frankie Fazul Jr. replied. "I never thought Vlactron *could*! I mean, he's *Luno Zorgoochi*!"

Concetta Cosmo agreed, stating that the guy was, like, *invincible*. Then she turned to Zoola Zeta, who was quietly shuffling along behind them, head cast down. Concetta barked at her to get a move on. Zoola looked up, snapping out of her funk, and picked up the pace.

The kids and their remaining parents, about three dozen in all, were safely aboard the barge. Since the automatic functions were turned off, Chooch had to manually pull up the heavy gangplank himself and once it clanked shut, he gave Clive the thumbs-up.

It was a long, tense journey to the Baccala Nebula, where the Quantum mother ship was moored. Chooch rocked back and forth, hugging the Luno Bot, muttering, "A life vest is located under your seat. When instructed to do so, slip it over your head, and then pass the straps around your waist and . . ."

This did not help the morale of the already-terrified adults and children, who certainly had every reason to be scared. They were just regular people trained to make pizza, not do battle with an intergalactic tyrant bent on taking over the galaxy.

The boys and girls sat grimly silent, holding back their tears as Connie, who was a Zorgoochi, but only through marriage, assumed leadership and told them that ever since Vlactron kidnapped the Pyramid,

Quantum has pretty much been the only pizza available in the spiral arm of the Mezzaluna Galaxy.

"If we don't fight back," she declared, "Vlactron will take over the rest of the galaxy with that artificial pizza of his and eventually the universe and we're not going to let that happen, *are we*?"

They all immediately stood up and shouted "NO!"

Then everyone recited the Pizza Pyramid Pledge: "We solemnly swear to make the best pizza, use only the freshest ingredients, and be a beacon of what is good and wholesome in the galaxy. PAX, AMORIS, PIZZA!"

The cabin was suddenly charged with the spirit to bravely fight for the two things they loved most in the universe: their family and pizza!

And they would need that bravery, too, because all they had to fight with was what they had to cook with: pizza cutters, large pizza paddles, ladles, pots, pans, etc.

Clive then gave an unnecessarily long-winded description of the layout of the Quantum mother ship, which was interrupted by Chooch, who assured them they had an ally in the small, but brave maintenance crew, the Arthropods. Then he asked if there was any pizza left because he was getting kind of hungry.

"Based upon our previous experience with Quantum," Clive said to Connie as they entered the Baccala Nebula and were drawing closer to the mother ship, "I was anticipating we would be required to have security clearance, but it appears for some reason, we do not."

The trash barge easily flew through the entranceway to the receiving bay and was soon touching down.

Chooch lowered the gangplank and then he and Clive hesitantly peeked out of the doorway. Chooch fearfully squeezed the Luno Bot.

"Not to worry, my comrades," Xoboz said, marching up the ramp with a confident snap in his step. "Vlactron's guards don't come down to the rubbish sector, especially for a routine porting of a trash barge."

Then Connie appeared in the doorway and Chooch introduced her as Luno's mother.

"It will be our honor to serve the most respected family in galactic pizza, Madame Zorgoochi!" Xoboz said, bowing deeply.

As they descended the gangplank, Xoboz told Clive and Chooch that after he and the Arthropods helped them escape the mother ship, it dawned on him that there were over 5,000 Arthropods, but only about 1,000 guards, yet the Quantum guards ruled over *them.*

"But that does not make sense," Clive said.

"Exactly!" Xoboz shouted. "Thanks to you two noble warriors, I remembered that I was once a great leader to my people!"

Xoboz then gestured to his Arthropod maintenance

crew now assembled in neat military rows before them, all proudly holding cleaning tools fashioned into weapons, ready for battle.

"I also remembered what a brave and powerful race we Arthropods are!" Xoboz said proudly, to which the Arthropods raised their weapons over their heads in perfect unison.

Connie asked Xoboz what his plan was to rescue the Pizza Pyramid.

"I knew I forgot something," Xoboz said, scratching his head.

Connie Zorgoochi smacked her forehead, rolled her eyes, and muttered, "Do I have to do *everything* myself?"

She looked around and spotted the Luno Bot that Chooch was holding and got an idea.

Right at that very moment in a cell several levels below, Luno was curled up on his bunk. He wasn't quite sleeping, but not quite awake either, just slowly sinking into a sea of despair and hopelessness. He began to sink even deeper when—

Screeeeeeek!

The sound of metal scraping against metal brought Luno back up to the surface of his consciousness.

He opened his eyes and squinted, then sat up and

blinked. It looked like the cell door had *opened*. He blinked a few more times and stared dumbly for a few more seconds before it sank in. The cell door *was* open.

He walked over and peeked out. The hallway was empty. *Was this a trap?* He didn't care. He might as well die trying to escape. For all he knew, his dad, mom, and everyone else could be dead by now anyway.

As Luno crept down the hall, he heard the echo of several more cell doors creak open, and to his surprise, other pizza delivery boys, girls, aliens, and robots cautiously peeked out.

"It's okay," Luno whispered. "I *think*."

As they gathered in the corridor, an alien delivery girl sporting a Proton Pizza uniform gasped at Luno.

"Hey!" she said. "You're *Luno Zorgoochi!*"

The others surrounded Luno, gaping at him and whispering things like *I heard about this guy* and *We're saved!*

Luno backed up as they all moved in closer, then bumped against a wall. He still couldn't figure out why anyone would think of him as a leader of *anything*, but he didn't have time to explain that he was no different from them. He pushed his way through the wide-eyed crowd and made his way to the far end of the hall. The others obediently followed him.

As he approached the thick metal door lined with

large rivets at the end of the hall, Luno wondered how he was going to open it, but before he could come up with a plan, it creaked open on its own just like his cell door. This was the case as he and the others moved through the complex network of corridors, slowly making their way to the upper levels of the mother ship.

Luno thought that he could very well be leading himself and even more innocent people to their doom, but felt that he was at least doing something and not just idly sitting in a cell.

"HALT!" a Quantum guard shouted several levels above Luno at that very moment.

Xoboz and a dozen of his crew stopped in their tracks. General Zope and a group of lower-ranking guards approached them.

"Who have you got there?" General Zope asked.

"We caught him in the rubbish sector," Xoboz replied.

"That's the human Zorgoochi!" one of the guards said. "Rex Vlactron had him locked up."

"He must've escaped through the trash chute in his cell," Xoboz said.

One of the guards reminded General Zope that the scanners had been malfunctioning for the last few days, which was probably how the human had gotten through undetected.

"What do you have to say for yourself, human, hmmm?" General Zope asked.

"I'm *fine*, Mom," Luno Bot droned. "Um, no thank you. I just want to sleep."

General Zope grabbed the Luno Bot by the arm, pulled him close, and sneered, "Oh, you'll sleep alright—*forever!*"

"I love you," the Luno Bot added.

"Obviously delirious," Xoboz said evenly.

General Zope turned to the other guards and said, "Rex Vlactron will be pleased that I single-handedly captured the human Zorgoochi!"

The guards gathered around, congratulating him.

"Oh, Arthropod," he sniffed, turning back and glancing down at Xoboz. "Back to your duties. We'll take over from here."

"No." Xoboz looked up and smiled. "*We* will."

The guards looked around.

They were surrounded by hundreds of very angry Arthropods, all brandishing makeshift weapons.

Before they could reach for theirs, General Zope and his guards were immediately swarmed by a race of noble creatures, which had suffered violence and humiliation from their masters for the very last time.

CHAPTER NINETEEN

The End of Real Pizza in the Universe?

"The entrance to the main kitchen is around that corner and at the end of the next hallway," Xoboz whispered, as he approached a turn in the corridor, but then stopped and put his finger to his lips.

Shhhh.

The Arthropods were poised, ready to strike down whatever was coming around that corner.

It grew closer and closer until . . .

"Hey! I—"

They lunged at someone or some*thing*, but before they could do any damage, Connie Zorgoochi swatted them away.

"Get off him, you idiots!" she shouted, plucking the Arthropods and tossing them away. "It's my *Luno!*"

She wrapped him in a tight embrace of sobs and kisses. Luno didn't know what was worse, the Arthropod attack or his mother.

"*Okay,* Mom," Luno finally said, wiping his face.

As soon as Connie stopped kissing him, she smacked him in the back of the head.

"You had me worried half sick!" she shouted. "I thought you were *dead!*"

"Well, if I was dead," said Luno, "then there'd be nothing you could do about it, so there'd be no point in worrying."

"Don't be a wise guy, mister," Connie said, and smacked him again.

Then she grabbed him and kissed him some more.

Luno barely had time to catch his breath when Chooch wrapped him in one of his bone-crushing group hugs with Clive, the Luno Bot, and a few delivery boys and girls, who weren't sure if they were being attacked.

Tony, Concetta, Frankie Boy Jr., and the rest of the Junior Pyramid members surrounded Luno and either hugged him or slapped him on the back to congratulate him. They said they just *knew* he'd outsmart Vlactron somehow, but when Luno tried to explain what really happened, they didn't seem to want to listen.

Once the reunion was over and they were all heading toward the doors to the Quantum kitchens, Luno felt a tap on his shoulder. He turned. It was Zoola Zeta.

"Oh, hi, Zoola," Luno said. "How are . . ."

She wrapped her arms around him and buried her face in his chest.

"Mmm fo apffy yoor hokay," she said into Luno's space suit.

"Huh?" Luno asked, trying to wriggle out of her embrace.

"I'm so happy you're okay," she said, looking up at him. "I was so *worried* about . . ."

"Let's *go*, you guys!" Concetta shouted. "*Move* it!"

Luno pried Zoola off as politely as he could and walked with the others, but everyone stopped cold at the sound of an echoing growl coming from down the hall followed by a wet *shlupp*ing sound, growing closer and closer.

Out of the shadows emerged two massive Mutant Calamari, wielding pizza cutter weapons!

Xoboz commanded his troops to attack and they did, completely covering the wailing creatures. However, after a few moments, Arthropods were flying every which way as the Calamari whipped their terrible tentacles around to shake them off.

Without time to think, Luno led the second wave of

attack, which was made all the more difficult by his mother trying to hold him back to keep him safe.

Once he wrestled himself free, Luno furiously poked and jabbed the squid creatures with one of the Arthropod's makeshift weapons, but after a few moments, he and the Junior Pyramid members and the delivery boys and girls discovered that they couldn't penetrate the Calamari's tough leathery hide.

Now having the upper tentacle, the Calamari advanced toward Luno and the rest, ready to shock them with their cutters or simply squeeze them to death in their atrocious appendages.

"Gak!" A tentacle wrapped around Luno's chest and lifted him into the air. Fortunately, his space suit protected him from direct contact with the Calamari, which would've triggered his allergies. But as fortunate as this was, he was still in big trouble. He dangled helplessly as the Calamari bellowed in anger, scooping up Arthropods and a few Junior Pyramid members.

Swink!

Luno hit the floor with the rest of them. He looked up and saw Zoola, panting, one foot on the floor and one on the now completely legless dead Calamari, holding a sharpened pizza paddle like a mighty sword.

"The base of the tentacle is the most tender part," she said, smiling. "And the most delicious!"

Luno blinked in disbelief. He unwound the dead tentacle from his waist and walked up to her. "I—um—"

"Well, it was going to hurt you," she said. "I had to do *something*. I . . ."

Suddenly they both flew into the air. Another Mutant Calamari had him, this time by the ankles and Zoola, too, and she dropped the pizza paddle. Luno futilely swung his fists as he dangled upside down trying to do something, *anything*, but it was no use.

The spinning blade of the Calamari's pizza cutter weapon glinted in Luno's eye. As it drew closer, he tried to wriggle free, but the tentacles were stuck fast. He

watched the shiny blade move steadily toward his throat.

Zoola gasped helplessly, watching.

"Luno!" she shouted. "Before we die, I need to tell you that I love—"

"EXTRA SHARP CHEDDAR, COMING THROUGH!"

The next thing Luno knew, he and Zoola were on the floor again. He looked up and saw the Calamari lying there next to them, sliced completely in two!

Luno pushed Zoola out of the way of a giant and very sharp wheel of yellowish cheese barreling back toward him.

"Hello, young Zorgoochi."

It was Master Uno and the Mozzarella Monks!

Luno got to his feet and Master Uno bowed deeply to him, so Luno bowed in return.

"Does *your* back hurt?" Master Uno asked, rubbing his back. "Bending down that way always makes me feel better, too."

Then Master Uno offered his hand and Luno shook it.

"Good to see you again." Master Uno smiled, helping him up.

As Clive and Chooch greeted the Monks, Luno approached Zoola.

"So, um," Luno muttered. "Were you going to say something before?"

"Uh, *yeah*." She laughed nervously. "I was going to say that I love, uh—*mozzarella*."

"Huh?"

"You say funny things when you think you're going to die," Zoola said, then quickly joined the others.

"So *you're* for real, too?" Connie asked Master Uno. "I thought you were a figment of my husband's crazy family's imagination."

"Hmmm." Master Uno considered this. "Perhaps I *am* and just exist in their minds, Madame. Perhaps we *all* do."

Connie looked over to Luno, who shook his head as if to say, *Never mind him.*

"Master Uno, how did you know I was here?" Luno asked. "And that we needed your help?"

"Ah, young Zorgoochi"—Master Uno smiled sagely— "I was practicing Transcend-Cheddar Meditation and sensed that you were in danger across the cold depths of space."

"Wow!" Luno gasped. "*Really?*"

"No," Master Uno said flatly. "We have one of those antennas, too."

There was a scuffle behind them and Luno turned around.

"What are you *doing*?" Due shouted at Nove, who was squeezing lemons and shaking salt and pepper on one of the Calamari's tentacles.

"It's getting close to lunchtime, so I was just thinking I could grill these up and . . ."

Due slapped the lemons out of his hands.

"How can you think of food at a time like this?" Due shouted, yanking Nove to his feet. "*C'mon!* Let's get that door open!"

The monks yanked at the heavy metal door of the kitchen, but it didn't creak open more than a fraction.

"Can *I* help?" Chooch asked, grasping the door handle and flinging it open wide, sending a few of the monks flying.

"Oops."

Luno, Connie, Clive, Chooch, and the rest gathered in the doorway and peered down upon the cavernous Quantum kitchen at the members of the Pizza Pyramid, using their talents in the service of Vlactron.

"Anthony!" Mrs. Galattico screamed as she ran down the stairs, her arms outstretched, followed by Tony.

Mr. Galattico spun around, dropped the basketball-size olive he was slicing, and ran to his wife and son. They hugged one another, then cried.

There was a mad rush of adults and kids down the stairs to the kitchen and another of pizza chefs toward them, resulting in a collision of kissing, sobbing, and shouting.

Connie and Luno ran down the steps, searching the crowd for Geo, but got caught in the jumble. Once he pulled himself free of Zoola Zeta and her parents' hugs, Luno found Mr. Galattico.

"Where's my father?" Luno asked Mr. Galattico, who tried to answer, but his wife was too busy kissing him. Once he pried her lips off, he managed to tell Luno that Geo was in the back room, and pointed toward a door.

Luno and Connie ran to the doorway.

They both froze.

"I guess I shoulda warned you first," Mr. Galattico said, catching up to them.

"Connie!" Geo squeaked. "Luno!"

"What did you do to my Geo?" Connie shrieked, running to her husband, who was standing on a table trying to roll out some dough.

He was no more than a foot and a half tall.

Regardless, Connie picked him up and hugged him and so did Luno.

"You should be proud of your husband, Connie," Mr. Fazul said.

"Why?" Connie snapped. "Because now I can buy a kid's ticket for him at the movies?"

Mr. Fazul explained that Vlactron ordered the Pyramid chefs to create a new size pizza that would be smaller than his already Extra Extra Unlarge. Being that Geo had experience making pizza for the microscopic universe of Parva, he decided to take on the task.

"That was one beautiful pie, even though you could only see it through an electron microscope," Mrs. Zeta said, patting Geo on the back, knocking him over.

"Then came time for the taste test," Mr. Fazul said, sadly shaking his head. "We had no idea there'd be any side effects when Geo volunteered."

"I stand behind every pizza I make!" Geo said proudly.

"Too bad nobody can see you when you do it now," Connie said.

"There's more bad news," Mr. Galattico said grimly.

"Worse than ordering from the children's menu for my husband for the rest of his life?" Connie snarled.

"He's getting *smaller*, Connie," Mrs. Zeta said, placing a hand on Connie's shoulder. "Pretty soon he's going to disappear *altogether*."

As Luno's mother collapsed into Mrs. Zeta's arms and wept, Geo asked Luno to pick him up.

"Don't worry about me, son," he said evenly. "Vlactron's gotta be stopped and as long as he doesn't have the Golden Anchovy, there's still a chance. *Capish?*"

Luno reluctantly told him he had handed the Golden Anchovy over in order to get him back, but then Vlactron double-crossed him and locked him up.

Geo smacked his forehead and cursed, "*Brutto Malo!*" but then quickly shook off the bad news.

"Okay, okay, there's *got* to be a way we can take him down," he said. "I got it! *Roog! He* can help us! Where is he?"

Luno then explained that Roog was secretly Vlactron's servant and he had double-crossed the Zorgoochi family.

"*Uffa!* After two centuries!" Geo said, then looked Luno square in the eye. "*Figlio mio,* my baby boy, it's all up to you now. The Pyramid will help, but it's up to *you* to stop Vlactron."

"But, *Dad . . .*"

"You already know what to do, Luno," Geo said evenly. "Now *do* it."

Once again, Luno wasn't sure if he really *did* know what to do, but nodded anyway.

"Okay, Dad," Luno said. "I won't let you d—"

"HOLD IT RIGHT THERE!" a voice shouted. "NO-BODY MOVE!"

Connie quickly stuffed her husband in her purse and slowly turned around.

A wall of Quantum Guards faced them with weapons drawn.

The highest-ranking guard stepped forward and said, "Rex Vlactron will be pleased that *I* single-handedly stopped this little rebellion of yours!"

Before his Reptilicon troops could congratulate

him, they froze where they stood. Then the row of icy guards fell forward, shattering into millions of pieces.

"Hey there, slush-a-roo!" smiled Frosto.

"We heard a friend of ours needed a little help," said Floe.

"Yeah, man," said Snowy Joey. "And anyone who would convert us into microscopic vapor in order to save us from oncoming meteors and then refreeze us into solid form is certainly a friend of ours!"

Sheldon hugged Luno. Delighted, Chooch scooped up Clive, a few Arthropods, and a couple of Junior Pyramid members and locked them all in a group hug.

"Thanks again for the big tip," Luno said to Frosto, "but it turned to water by the time I got home."

"That's the thing about Freezorg money," said Frosto. "You have to spend it before it melts!"

"So what do you want us to do, Luno?" Snowy Joey asked as everyone gathered round.

"We need to find the Golden Anchovy!" Luno announced. "There's a chance that Vlactron hasn't touched it yet."

Before Clive could calculate the astronomical odds against that possibility, Luno instructed everyone to break up into groups to look for it, but arm themselves just in case they encountered any guards or Mutant Calamari.

"Now does anyone have any questions?" Luno asked.

"Yes," said Connie. "are you wearing clean underwear?"

"*Mom!*" Luno shouted in disbelief as the crowd dispersed.

Luno stood in the corner of the kitchen, watching everyone form into teams and then courageously march off into battle for the fate of the galaxy. He drew a heavy sigh, suddenly feeling the gravity of what was at stake. His shoulders slumped, but then he realized it was because Chooch's giant metal hand was on it.

"Can Clive and I go with *you*, Luno?" Chooch asked.

"I can observe the plumbing system along the way, Mr. Zorgoochi," added Clive.

"Sure," Luno replied and they started off, but turned when he heard his name called.

"Where do you think *you're* going?" Connie asked, rushing up to him.

"Clive, Chooch, and I are going to find the Golden Anchovy," Luno replied.

"Oh, *really*?" Connie snapped. "Well, I hate to tell you this, but you've been grounded for sneaking out of the house, so you're not going *anywhere*!"

"Connie!" Geo's head popped out of her purse. "Let the kid go! He's gotta do this!"

"Alright then," she said. "But I'm coming with you!"

"*What?*" Luno shouted.

"He's gotta do this on his *own*, Connie," Geo said.

Connie told him to be quiet and pushed him back into her purse. She snapped it shut, but Geo kept shouting.

"Mom," said Luno, "I can do this."

Connie looked down and brushed away a tear, then looked back up and pushed the hair out of Luno's eyes.

"I know, sweetheart," she said. "I guess I forget you're not a little boy anymore."

She kissed him on the forehead and told him to be safe. Luno turned and began to walk away.

"Are you chilly, honey?" she asked. "Because I brought you a sweater just in case."

"No thanks, Mom," Luno sighed and started up the stairs.

Then she pulled Clive and Chooch aside.

"Listen, you two," she whispered, "if you let *anything* happen to my baby, *you're* going to find yourself sold for spare parts and *you're* going to find yourself on a loaf of garlic bread."

Chooch gulped and Clive blinked, but they both understood. Then they quickly climbed the stairs to catch up with Luno.

They walked through eerily empty corridors, hearing vague far-off shouts, crashes, and explosions. The battle had already begun. Chooch clutched Luno's arm until it was numb, while Clive calmly scanned the perimeter with his device.

"We are approaching the receiving bay, Mr. Zorgoochi," Clive informed Luno. "There will be transporters to take us to the uppermost levels, where Vlactron's private chamber is located."

"Thanks, Clive," said Luno.

"However, if we turn left at this next junction," said Clive, "we will have an excellent opportunity to observe the plumbing system's ingeniously designed auxiliary water filtration station, which is . . ."

"*Not* a good time, Clive," groaned Luno.

They came to the end of the corridor and cautiously peeked out into the landing area, which was littered with unconscious guards.

As they crept along, a transporter silently descended from above and landed before them almost as if it was waiting for their arrival. Luno looked to Clive and Chooch, shrugged, and they climbed aboard.

"Destination, please," requested a small female voice.

"Vlactron's private lair?" Luno asked hopefully.

They zoomed to the very highest reaches of the mother ship with such velocity that it caused a few of Chooch's more important parts to come loose.

Along the way, Luno could see skirmishes on several levels between the Quantum guards and Mutant Calamari and the Senior and Junior Pyramid members, Arthropods, the Mozzarella Monks, and even the Freezorgs. Luno wanted to stop and join the battle, or at least find out if his parents were okay, but kept going.

By the time they slowed to a stop, Clive had put Chooch back together.

They stepped off the transporter and headed down a long dark corridor with a giant black door at the end. But this time, there were no Calamari guarding it.

Luno slowly pushed the door open and stuck his head in. He scanned the room, but there was no one. Then he spotted it among display cases of Vlactron's skeleton trophies: the Golden Anchovy!

As Luno approached, he noticed it was no longer in the tomato sauce jar, but in an ornate crystal decanter, its top screwed on tight, adorned with small horned lizards carved around its base, resting on a pedestal. As he watched his own hand reach out, Luno felt his heart beat through his space suit.

"Hello, Illuminato," a voice said softly.

Vlactron emerged from the shadows, his cape flowing behind him.

"So good of you to visit me once again," Vlactron said, yellow eyes blazing through the darkness. "And I hear that your friends and family have come to visit me as well."

Luno looked at the Golden Anchovy, which now appeared to have lost its glow as it swam lethargically around the bowl. Luno thought that perhaps it somehow knew what it was going to be used for next.

"I see you've come for one last look at the Golden Anchovy before I use it to fulfill my grand vision of total domination of pizza throughout the universe," Vlactron said. "My only regret is that you won't live long enough to witness the fulfillment of my destiny."

Luno swallowed hard. He could hear Chooch rattling with fear and Clive pecking away at his device behind him.

"Or perhaps you *will* in a way," Vlactron said, gesturing toward an empty display case with a plaque with the word "human" engraved on it.

"Quantum Pizza is *bad*," Luno finally spoke. "There'll always be people who won't eat it."

"Once I destroy every other pizzeria in the galaxy," Vlactron said, smiling, "they'll *have* to."

"But they'll fight back!" Luno shouted. "They'll make their *own*!"

Vlactron chuckled, then calmly explained that no one could possibly make their own if *he* controlled all of the ingredients, but even if they tried, he would soon own the molecular formula of pizza itself!

"And then it will be punishable by death for anyone

to make pizza except *me*." Vlactron smiled blithely at what he was saying, then snapped out of it. "Calamari!"

Luno suddenly felt clammy tentacles slither around his arms and waist.

"To the cheese room!" Vlactron commanded, grabbing the decanter. He pushed Clive and Chooch out of the way and strutted out of the room. The Calamari followed, dragging Luno and growling menacingly at Chooch when he tried to reach out for Luno.

They boarded a waiting transporter, and as they began to descend, Luno could hear Chooch cry his name.

"All of this may very well soon be destroyed, but it's served its purpose," Vlactron mused, clutching the crystal decanter and looking around at the dozens of battles exploding on every level. "Just like your species, it too will come to an end now that its function is complete. Being that Earth was destroyed centuries ago, the only thing left to mark humanity's tiny existence other than your very bones on display among my trophies will be *pizza*. But in time, its creation will be attributed to *me* and no one will even remember who the Zorgoochis were. More time shall pass and your very species will be extinct and forgotten. It will be as if humanity never even existed."

The transporter slowed to a stop.

Vlactron marched ahead as the Calamari's tentacles yanked Luno forward. They entered the cheese room and Vlactron climbed up a flight of stairs to a catwalk directly over several massive vats of curds and whey in the process of being separated. The Calamari dragged Luno up the stairs and dangled him over one of the churning vats.

"Real pizza will never die," Luno wheezed, barely able to breathe with the tentacle wrapped tightly around his chest. "You won't win."

"I already *have*." Vlactron leaned in close. "Pizza is *mine* and so is the Golden Anchovy."

Vlactron then turned to one of the Calamari and told it to prepare his escape pod located behind the pizza prep room several levels above. He descended the stairs and almost as an afterthought added, "Oh, and dispose of the human."

Luno held his breath as he plunged into the colossal vat of warm liquid. He thrashed about, trying to keep his head above water and search for the edges. The rising steam from the milk veiled his surroundings, disorienting him.

"Help!" Luno gasped. "Somebody!"

But no one heard him.

Luno knew he couldn't keep this up much longer. His muscles were aching. Each time he went under, it took increasingly more and more effort to pull himself back to the surface.

He found himself sinking once again, but just didn't have enough strength to come back up.

Luno hit bottom.

And stayed there.

How could stupid little me think I could defeat the biggest, most powerful alien in the galaxy?

Luno was tired of fighting. Tired of trying. Tired of losing.

He was just *tired*.

"I'm sorry, Dad," Luno said, as a bubble filled with his last bit of oxygen floated to the surface and popped.

CHAPTER TWENTY

The Final Battle

"Wa-hoo!" Geo shouted as he squeezed the trigger with both of his tiny hands, firing olive pits at a battalion of Quantum guards. Thanks to a little mechanical tinkering on his part, rather than olives, the atomic olive pitter now shot the *pits*. As an added bonus, these were piccante olives, which had a combustible stone, so they exploded upon impact.

"Hey, Connie!" the diminutive dad chirped. "Load me up with more olives! I can't reach the jar!"

The receiving bay was in total chaos. Troops of Quantum guards rushed back and forth across the massive platform, weapons drawn, attacking the Pizza Pyramid, who shielded themselves with titanium pizza trays. Hijacked transporters whirred overhead, piloted by several delivery boys and girls who dumped tomato sauce so spicy over the side it ate into the guards' battle armor.

Frankie Fazul Sr. and his son, Frankie Boy, led an attack, thrusting the pizza cutter weapons at the guards, pushing them back farther and farther. Concetta Cosmo heroically launched pound after pound of super-sticky globs of mozzarella at the guards, immobilizing them in the glutinous goo.

And where there weren't Pyramid members, there were Arthropods battling it out. They may have been small, but they were stout of heart.

"Arthropods *attack*!" Xoboz gave the battle cry, commanding his troops to swarm over Vlactron's forces and strip them of their protective gear. En masse, the Arthropods would then carry the guards, deposit them into the dumpsters, and rivet them shut.

"Nice shot, sweetie!" Mrs. Zeta complimented her daughter, Zoola, when she sent a dozen flaming bowling-ball-size meatballs into an advancing squadron of guards, scattering them in every direction.

"Thanks, Mom," Zoola replied, hugging her parents.

Even Mr. Cosmo and Mr. Galattico, who both laid claim to being the first to invent the antigravity pizza, set aside their long-standing feud and bravely fought side by side against Vlactron's troops.

"Squeee!" a herd of Mutant Calamari shrieked as they led an assault on the Pizza Pyramid's stronghold.

Connie grabbed Geo, who was still gleefully shooting olive pits, and ran for cover, along with several other Pyramid members.

"Well, this is just *great*," said Connie, watching the Calamari advance toward their barricade of piled-up pizza ovens, dough mixers, and massive saucepots. "We're cornered and there's no way out. I blame you and your crazy family for all of this! I'll never forgive you, Geo Zorgoochi, for as long as I live, which looks like it will be about twenty seconds."

"I love you, too, sweetheart," Geo said, then stood on his tiptoes and kissed her.

"*Grraaahhh!*"

Peeking over their barricade, they saw a massive greenish-blue-veined creature plucking off the helpless Calamari's tentacles one by one.

"Nice work, boys," Master Uno congratulated the Mozzarella Monks, who were standing by, proudly watching the proceedings.

Master Uno walked over to Connie and extended a hand.

"I hope you're unharmed and hungry, Madame," Master Uno said, helping Connie to her feet. "Once that Gorgonzola Gorgon the monks and I whipped up is through with those Calamari, it'll make a tasty snack."

"I brought the crackers!" added Nove.

There were skirmishes in each and every sector. Explosions erupted everywhere. Debris rained down, walls crumbled, and floors shook. The Quantum mother ship was aflame with war and was slowly dying, piece by piece.

As the sounds of battle echoed throughout the network of secret corridors, Vlactron walked swiftly through on

his way to his private transporter to take him to a chamber behind the pizza prep room, where his escape pod was waiting.

Clutching the sloshing decanter containing the Golden Anchovy, he puzzled over how enemy forces could've infiltrated his ship with such tight security. However, he soon turned to a plan growing in his Reptilicon brain: He would safely flee the mother ship before it was entirely destroyed. Then he would finally take possession of the Golden Anchovy and fulfill his destiny of wielding absolute control over pizza in the universe. But first he would need to safely make it to his escape pod.

Vlactron came to a stop and creaked open a small hidden door that led to his personal transporter, but let out a barrage of curses when he discovered that a collapsed ceiling had destroyed it. He refused to let such a minor setback stop him, so he immediately ran to the main transporter causeway. As far as he was concerned, he was *already* under the protection of the Golden Anchovy simply because it was his divine right to possess it. It was just a mere technicality that he would have to touch it with his bare claws.

Vlactron flung open the door leading to the causeway and marched to a waiting transporter, which one of his guards was about to take into battle.

"Rex Vlactron, sir!" the surprised young guard exclaimed, standing at attention holding his pizza cutter weapon at his side, and saluting. "It would be my honor to transport you to a safe location, sir, but at the present time, it may be too dangerous, so I . . ."

Without speaking, Vlactron snatched the weapon from the confused guard's hand and jabbed him. He immediately crumpled to the floor, and Vlactron kicked him aside, climbed into the pilot's seat, and zoomed off.

As he soared above the raging battle, Vlactron's transporter was not hit, deepening his profound belief that it truly was his destiny to be the pizza master of the universe. Within moments, he arrived at the pizza prep level and hopped out.

Vlactron hardly noticed his entire empire crumbling around him as he stepped over faithful fallen guards. He swiftly marched down the hallway to the secret entrance, which led to the escape pod chamber.

As Vlactron grew closer, he slowed down and expelled a hot angry breath at the sight of the door sealed up by fallen debris. Without hesitation, he spun on his heel and began to make the long walk around to the pizza prep room, where he had wisely made sure the mother ship's architects created another well-hidden door to the escape pod chamber as well.

Clive and Chooch walked around aimlessly.

"Due to the sporadic surges in the **Quantum** mother ship's radioactive signal," said Clive, poking futilely at his gadget, "my multiphase subatomic analytical device is not capable of locating the cheese room where Mr. Zorgoochi is said to be located."

Clive sat down on a hunk of debris and placed his device next to him.

"What're you *doing*?" Chooch asked, tugging Clive's sleeve. "We gotta keep looking for Luno!"

"The numerical odds against Mr. Zorgoochi currently being alive are so astronomically high, it would require the invention of a new number," said Clive, looking down at a pool of water forming at his feet. "Hmmm. There seems to be clear liquid discharging from my eyes. Have I sprung a leak, Chooch?"

"You're *crying*, Clive." Chooch smiled sadly, putting an arm around him. "It means you love Luno, too, but it also means *we can't give up*!"

"But Mr. Zorgoochi is gone," said Clive, tears pouring down his face. "I just *feel* it."

"That is entirely unsound, extremely unfounded, and highly unscientific," Chooch said.

"Then what do we *do*?" Clive asked.

"We keep looking!" said Chooch and hugged Clive, but then their embrace grew tighter until they were both gasping for air and Chooch's titanium body began to buckle under the pressure like a tin can.

They finally realized that a Mutant Calamari had them in its tentacles and was squeezing them to death.

Several levels below, the cheese room was silent and still, except for the distant echo of battle, which made slight ripples on the surface of the liquid in one of the massive vats.

Resting at the bottom, Luno gazed at the curds lazily floating above him, imagining they were his ancestors' faces. They looked down at him through the muted light.

Soon this will all be over, Luno thought, *just as Vlactron said it would. All things must come to an end, even the human race.*

And it's all my fault.

Luno thought that maybe his mother was right: The Zorgoochis were a bunch of kooks who took pizza entirely too seriously.

He watched his great-grandparents, aunts, uncles, and cousins swirling above him. Generation after generation of working hard, sacrificing, and even facing death—for what?

Pizza?

It was just something to eat—or *was* it?

The happiest times in Luno's life were when he was eating pizza with his family. He knew that Zorgoochi Intergalactic Pizza certainly delivered happiness by the slice throughout the galaxy. And didn't the Galactic Declaration of Independence state that all humans, sentient masses of protons, and aliens have unalienable rights, like life, liberty, and the pursuit of *happiness*?

He also knew that no one should be able to take anyone's happiness away, no matter how big and powerful they were. And shouldn't everyone be able to have a choice of any kind of pizza they wanted—like thick or thin crust? Wasn't that in the Peace of Pizza Treaty that was signed at the end of the Great Pizza War?

So maybe this isn't just about me, Luno thought. *Maybe it's bigger.*

Bigger than the Zorgoochis.

Bigger than pizza.

He watched the curds separate from the whey.

Then Geo's voice echoed in Luno's head.

You already know what to do. Now do it.

Luno had heard those words his whole life, but not until this very moment did he truly understand them.

He pulled away from the bottom of the vat, rising past his ancestors, toward the light, and up to the surface.

His nose hit the air first. He inhaled deeply, filling

his lungs, then looked up and saw something dangling from the ceiling above him.

It was a strand of string cheese.

Luno didn't bother questioning how it got there. He just reached up and pulled himself out of the vat. Dripping wet, he swung back and forth and jumped, landing with a *squish* on the floor.

Once he caught his breath, he stood up. Now full of bravery and purpose, Luno bounded out of the room to join the fight.

Unfortunately the bottoms of his boots were covered with cheese curds, and he slipped head over heels and fell on his backside.

Clive and Chooch were slowly being crushed together when the Calamari suddenly let out an ear-piercing screech. It released its tentacles and scurried out of the room.

"Now, why didn't I think of this before?" Luno said, sauntering up to them, smelling of cheese and holding a watermelon-size lemon wedge in one hand and a bucket of marinara sauce in the other. "Calamari naturally flee from their condiments for fear of being eaten!"

Delighted, Chooch insisted on a group hug, even though the last one had nearly killed them.

Luno armed Clive and Chooch with giant lemon

wedges and sauce and sent them down a corridor to flush out more Calamari while he did the same in the other direction.

Luno heard several crashes coming from the pizza prep room down the hall, so he sidled up to the doorway and peeked in. He crept toward the sound and around rows of massive vats of rising pizza dough, then looked up. At the far end of a rickety catwalk was Vlactron, alone, desperately trying to clear away fallen debris blocking a partially exposed door.

"How could you do it, Vlactron?" Luno shouted.

"Zorgoochi!" Vlactron snarled as he spun around. "You're supposed to be *dead*!"

Vlactron then looked down at Luno, so tiny among the massive dough vats in the cavernous room, and snickered, "A small detail I will tend to."

"Solaro treated you like *family*," Luno said. "He taught you everything you know about pizza."

"W-who told you that?" Vlactron wheeled back.

"Ha! I know *everything*!" Luno shouted. "How he trained you and was even going to leave you his pizzeria!"

"That's a *lie*!" Vlactron leaned in. "I created all of this by myself! Solaro Zorgoochi had nothing to do with it."

"You didn't even care about pizza at all, just the Golden Anchovy!" Luno shouted. "You're not interested in giving people something that tastes good and is made out of real ingredients. Your pizza is full of chemicals and tastes *awful!*"

"This is not about *pizza*, you insignificant human! It's about *power!*" Vlactron pounded his chest with a clenched fist. "And it doesn't matter any longer because the Golden Anchovy now belongs to *me!*"

"It can't belong to anyone," said Luno, remembering what Solaro said 200 years ago. "The Golden Anchovy belongs to the *universe.*"

"But *I* am worthy of its power and your ancestor was *not*," Vlactron replied. "Therefore it is rightfully *mine.*"

"Well, if it's rightfully yours, then why didn't he give it to you," Luno said, "or why couldn't you find it yourself?"

Vlactron's eyes narrowed and his tail switched angrily.

"Or maybe only a *Zorgoochi* was meant to find it?" Luno asked, tapping the side of his nose.

Vlactron seethed with anger at Luno. Then the two of them turned to the decanter containing the Golden Anchovy resting on the far end of the catwalk. They turned back to each other and a wide grin grew on Vlactron's crooked mouth.

At the exact same moment, both Luno and Vlactron bolted toward it. Luno took the stairs three at a time as Vlactron thundered across the narrow platform.

Vlactron got there first and picked up the decanter. He unscrewed the lid and ripped off his glove, exposing a horrible reptilian claw.

"You cannot stop me from fulfilling my destiny!" he bellowed.

Luno raced across the platform, then leapt into the air, but Vlactron swatted him away with his tail.

Luno quickly recovered and used every pizza-making move Roog had ever taught him. Chop! Slice! Spin! But Vlactron held on to the decanter tightly as his claw chased the terrified Golden Anchovy around and around the sloshing water while warding Luno off.

Luno feared harming the Golden Anchovy, but knew that a universe without it was far better than a universe with only Quantum Pizza, so he did the only thing he could think of.

Luno drew his leg back and, with all his might, kicked the bottom of the decanter, sending it into the air. He toppled off the platform and landed on a massive pile of pizza dough with a *squish*.

Agape, both Luno and Vlactron watched the decanter spinning above them. As if in slow motion, the Anchovy tumbled out and Vlactron reached over the railing as far as his arms could stretch, but it wasn't far enough. The Golden Anchovy was about to hit the floor.

Luno ran directly under the Golden Anchovy with his hands open above his head and looked up,

determined to catch it. But he slipped on some dough.

The room was silent as Luno hit the floor, landing on a pile of dough. Then he let out a loud resounding *bluuurp*.

Instead of catching the Golden Anchovy, Luno *swallowed* it.

"You foolish human!" Vlactron roared, bounding toward the stairs, the platform reverberating with every step. "I am going to rip it out of you with my bare claws! The Golden Anchovy belongs to *me!*"

Luno backed up, screwed his eyes shut, and dug his fingers into the pizza dough. He tore off a hunk and kneaded faster than he ever had in his life. As Vlactron's boot hit the first step, Luno gulped hard and performed the Zorgoochi Pizza Toss, sending the dough spinning into the air toward Vlactron so fast it was just a blur.

Bull's-eye! It hit Vlactron right in the knees, knocking him head over tail into one of the massive vats of pizza dough.

"Aaarrrggghhh!" Vlactron shouted, his cyber eye rolling up into his head as the dough swallowed him up like a giant calzone of death. "You cannot stop me, Zorgoochi! I will possess the Golden Anchovy! It is my destin . . ."

GLOOP!

"Hey, Luno!" Chooch shouted, as he and Clive ran up to him. "Are you okay? We heard lots of noise and somebody yelling and—"

"I'm fine," Luno said, rubbing the top of his head and clutching his chest. "I . . ."

Luno's head felt all tingly and his lungs felt funny.

"I . . ." Luno tried to talk again, now short of breath and light-headed.

Chooch placed his hand on Luno's shoulder as Clive scanned him with his device, attempting to determine why Luno appeared to be malfunctioning.

Then it dawned on Luno as he sat down on the floor: *the Golden Anchovy!*

He lay on his back, trying to comprehend that he was about to have the same mystical experience his great-great-great-great-great-grandfather Solaro Zorgoochi had so many years ago.

Luno could feel the energy of the universe surging through him. He understood that the Golden Anchovy was just raw power and it all depended on what it was used for, so he flooded his mind with positive things: peace; love; a nice hot pizza, fresh out of the oven.

Okay, Luno thought. *Here it comes.*

But nothing.

"Um, are you *okay*, Luno?" asked Chooch.

"Ri ro ro," Luno managed to say through a swollen tongue and waves of nausea.

"QUANTUM HAS BEEN DEFEATED!" a voice shouted as a cheering crowd burst into the pizza prep room. "Pizza is saved!"

They walked up and gathered around Luno, Clive, and Chooch.

Zoola choked back a gasp when she saw him lying on the floor. "Luno . . ."

Connie pushed her way through to the front.

"What did you do to my baby?!" she shrieked, kneeling next to him, stroking his hair.

"He swallowed the Golden Anchovy," Chooch explained.

"Stand back, everybody!" Geo shouted, emerging from a forest of legs. "The power and might of the Golden Anchovy is kicking in!"

Connie felt Luno's pulse and then put an ear to his chest. Then she quickly took out an allergy pen from her purse.

"The power and might of your son's *seafood allergy* is kicking in, you *gagutz*!" she said, pulling the cap off with her teeth and sinking the needle into his leg.

Everyone silently watched Luno just lie there, wheezing and turning purple.

Connie held Luno's hand, and Geo's tiny hand

clasped his other one. Then Luno's parents held hands and watched over their son.

After an agonizing minute, Luno's eyes fluttered open and he inhaled deeply. He coughed a few times and Connie sat him up. Everyone let out a collective sigh of relief.

"How are you, son?" Geo asked, reaching up and patting him on the back.

"Ahm oo-kay," Luno replied, catching his breath. "I tink da swelling's goin' down."

"Are you hungry, sweetheart?" Connie asked. "Because I think I have some *pizzelles* in my bag."

"No tonks, Mom." Luno sighed.

After a few more minutes, Connie helped Luno to his feet. His color returned and he was breathing normally again.

"I don't get it," said Luno. "I swallowed the Golden Anchovy and *nothing happened!*"

"Dat iz becauze it vas fake." Roog appeared in the doorway, holding up the very much alive and happily glowing Golden Anchovy, in a tomato sauce jar. "*I* have *real* vun."

Roog entered the room followed by dozens of Arthropods, warily aiming their weapons at him, ready to strike if he made a move to harm anyone.

"Hello Roog." Quattro sneered as he passed the Mozzarella Monks. "It's been a long time."

Roog looked down and grunted *hullo.*

"How's the *claw*?" Tre glowered.

Roog ignored them and marched on.

"We found him in a cell when we were releasing the rest of Vlactron's prisoners." Xoboz marched up to Geo and saluted. "He insisted on talking to you."

"Oh, so now that Vlactron's been defeated," said Luno, "you want to come back to *our* side?"

"Roog," said Geo. "How could you betray us?"

"We treated you like one of the family," Connie said, holding back tears.

"Pleeze tell leetle bugs to vithdraw veapons, Mr. Z," Roog asked. "And I vill hexplain."

Dad gave Xoboz a nod and he ordered his troops to stand down. Roog approached the Zorgoochis.

"Eet ees true I vas on Wlactron's zide," Roog sighed. "But dat vas many years ago."

Roog explained that after Solaro retired from traveling the galaxy on his mission of Peace, Love, and Pizza and founded Zorgoochi Intergalactic Pizza, he hired Roog. Not long after that, he took on a promising young apprentice, an eager Reptilicon named Vlactron.

Solaro taught the apprentice everything he knew about pizza, and his talented pupil learned quickly. Solaro even considered passing his pizzeria and eventually the Golden Anchovy on to Vlactron when he retired.

But what Solaro *didn't* know was that this bright,

hard-working, and seemingly loyal student was only interested in one thing: the Golden Anchovy.

While Vlactron worked down in the kitchen, he confided in Roog his grand plans of one day taking over Zorgoochi Intergalactic Pizza and turning it into a franchise throughout the Mezzaluna Galaxy, and ultimately the universe, making him the most successful and powerful pizzeria owner ever.

All he needed was the Golden Anchovy.

"At dat moment," Roog regretfully confessed, "I svitched allegiance to Wlactron. He promise me position of right-hand man vhen he took over pizzeria."

Solaro started to become suspicious of Vlactron when he began to ask less questions about pizza and more about the Golden Anchovy. It didn't take very long before Solaro changed his mind about who he would leave his pizzeria to. His son.

When Solaro told Vlactron he wasn't giving him the Anchovy, but rather that he hid it, Vlactron stormed off vowing he would someday destroy Zorgoochi Intergalactic Pizza, possess the Golden Anchovy, and rule the universe.

Vlactron was gone for many years, but Roog continued to work for the Zorgoochis, loyally waiting for Vlactron's return. However, in that time, through the love and kindness of the Zorgoochis, Roog became a trusted employee and his loyalty switched to them. He eventually became a beloved family friend, training generation after generation the secrets of pizza making.

"I never had family," Roog said, eyes cast downward. "*Zorgoochi* vas now my family."

Years later, when Vlactron was indeed the most successful and powerful pizzeria owner ever, he secretly contacted Roog. He still wanted the Golden Anchovy, which by then had been hidden by Solaro from even his own family for many years for fear of putting them in danger. Solaro claimed that only a Zorgoochi could find it.

Roog continued his charade of loyalty to Vlactron because he knew that by then the Zorgoochis would never be able to defeat him without the Golden Anchovy. Roog cleverly managed to forestall Vlactron from destroying Zorgoochi Intergalactic Pizza by promising him that one day a suitable Zorgoochi would be born who would be able to find it. This also bought Roog time to find it first, but he failed.

"Wlactron vas growing impatient and vanted to destroy Zorgoochi." Roog sighed. "Zo I told him vhen Luno vas young boy dat he vould be de vun to find Anchowy."

"But how did you know I would?" Luno asked.

"Becauze you haff same zuper-zenzative noze like Solaro," Roog replied. "Dat ees vhy I train you harder den all udder Zorgoochi. You *hed* to be de vun. Bezides, time and Wlactron's patience vas running out."

Now all that was needed was a good enough reason for Luno to find it. Roog knew Luno loved his father, so he planted the idea in Vlactron's head of holding Geo Zorgoochi for ransom in exchange for the Golden Anchovy.

"How could you do such a thing, Roog?" Connie shouted.

"Because, Mrs. Z, I knew dat Mr. Z and rest of Pyramid vould be safer verking for Wlactron on mudder ship den in der own pizzeria."

Connie reluctantly admitted that once the Pyramid members were kidnapped, the attacks on pizzerias ceased and the members were all indeed unharmed. Well, except for Geo. The pizzerias couldn't function without them, but Roog argued that "dey ver steel zafe becauze Wlactron needed dem to verk for him."

To Roog's relief, Luno located the Golden Anchovy. However, on the way to the Quantum mother ship, Roog pocketed the real one and gave Luno a fake to unwittingly deliver to Vlactron, who had never actually seen it, so wouldn't have known if it was the real one or not.

Then Roog's plan was to hold off Vlactron from using it or discovering it was a phony long enough to get the real Golden Anchovy, Geo, Luno, and himself back to Industro12 to figure out their next move, but Vlactron became suspicious of Roog's loyalty and imprisoned him.

"I don't get it," Luno said to Roog. "Why didn't *you* just hold the Golden Anchovy yourself?"

"No, no, no," Roog said, looking down. "Roog iz not vorthy of such ting."

"Well, then why didn't you tell me to hold the Golden Anchovy when I found it in the pond behind the pizzeria?" Luno asked.

"*Vhy?*" Roog chuckled, handing the jar down to Geo. "Becauze, boy, you are not ready yet."

"You're right, Roog, but maybe Luno is ready to *protect* it," said Geo, handing the jar up to Luno, who slipped it into his pocket.

"I'm sorry I doubted you, Roog," Luno said, shaking Roog's old crusty claw, but then it turned into a hug.

"Do I still haff job at pizzeria?" Roog asked sheepishly.

"For as long as you want," said Connie, reaching out and hugging him, which Chooch then turned into a group hug.

"When life gives you lemonade," sighed Chooch, "you . . . um . . ."

"Who wants pizza?" Geo shouted, to which there was a resounding "me!"

As everyone made their way back to the trash barge, Geo looked up at Luno.

"So how *did* you bring down Vlactron anyway?" he asked.

"Oh, I just used the old Zorgoochi Pizza Toss!" Luno smiled.

"I'm so *proud* of you, son!" Geo said with a twinkle in his eye as he hugged Luno's knees.

As Luno trailed behind the happy crowd, he heard

a sound so small he wasn't sure he heard it at first. He went to investigate.

It became louder as he approached a half-open door, which gave a soft creak as Luno pushed it open.

Behind a massive control panel, surrounded by dozens of static-filled monitors, sat a small figure, her back to Luno. She was crying.

"Um, excuse me," Luno said, gently placing his hand on her shoulder. "Are you um, *okay?*"

When she spun around, Luno saw that she was a Reptilicon, just like Vlactron and his guards, but she was different from them. The first thing Luno noticed was her eyes, so big and yellow, and full of tears. The second thing was that she had a slight aroma of string cheese.

"Oh, I-I'm sorry," she said. "I didn't realize anyone else was left on the ship. Alive, I mean. I thought I was *all alone.*"

"Um, well, we were all just kinda leaving," Luno said. "I—um, I'm Luno."

He awkwardly offered his hand for her to shake.

"Oh, I know who *you* are, Luno," she replied. "You're the human boy who had that silver scungilli thingie."

"Golden Anchovy," Luno corrected her.

"I'm Elvina." She smiled, placing her small soft claw in his hand.

Luno pulled his clammy hand away and wiped it on his space suit, embarrassed.

"I'm not sure if it would do any good for me to apologize for Vlactron," Elvina said. "He may have been an evil, bloodthirsty, tyrannical warlord hell-bent on controlling pizza throughout the universe and wouldn't think twice about murdering anyone in cold blood who stood in his way, but, you see, he was my uncle and the only one left in the universe to look after me since my father . . ."

Elvina burst into tears and buried her face in Luno's chest, sobbing. Luno had absolutely no idea what to do. He just waited for her to stop.

Once recovered, Elvina explained that she never knew her mother and then her father had died a few years ago, so when she was old enough, she searched the galaxy for her only known living relative, her father's brother, Vlactron. Elvina lamented that ever since, she'd led a lonely life, living on the Quantum mother ship under the thumb of her evil uncle.

"And now I have *no one*."—she sniffed—"I face this cold, dark universe *alone*."

You know what to do, Luno thought. *Now* do *it*.

"Um, would you," Luno stammered, "like to, um, stay with me and my family? I mean, until you . . ."

"I'd *love* to!" Elvina squealed, hugging him, and then cried some more.

And Luno thought this would get her to *stop* crying.

"Luno!" Connie's voice echoed in the hallway.

"In *here*, Mom!" Luno called.

Luno's parents appeared in the doorway with the rest behind them.

"We're ready to go," Connie said, then noticed Elvina. "And who is this?"

As the crowd gathered around the doorway, Luno explained that she was Vlactron's niece, who was practically held prisoner on the Quantum mother ship and that she was now an orphan.

"*Again*," Elvina added.

"You poor thing," Connie said, caressing Elvina's scaly cheek with her palm.

"She doesn't have anybody or anywhere to go," Luno said. "Could she stay with us?"

Without a moment's hesitation, Connie agreed and then she and Elvina hugged.

"At last," Elvina choked through her tears, "I have a real family!"

"At last," said Connie, "I have a daughter!"

Geo reached up and managed to hug her kneecaps, but Roog kept his distance, muttering, "Yes, yes, velcome to family." Then Elvina reached out to Luno and gave him the biggest hug of all.

"But, *Luno*," Zoola gasped as she pushed her way through the crowd, "she's a Reptilicon, just like *Vlactron!*"

Elvina narrowed her eyes at Zoola and her tail

switched back and forth, but then she turned to Luno and began bawling again in his arms, while elbowing Zoola out of the way.

"I-I can't help what species I am!" Elvina blubbered.

"Oh, she didn't mean anything," Connie said, patting Elvina on the back. "Do you like lasagna, sweetheart?"

"Oh, yes, Mrs. Zorgoochi," Elvina sniffled.

"Call me *Mom*," she said.

"Okay"—giggled Elvina—"*Mom!*"

Neither Luno nor anyone else saw Elvina smack Zoola with her tail as she and Connie went off to pack her bags.

Geo poked Luno's leg.

"That was a kind thing you did, son," Geo said proudly. "You have a good heart."

"Yeah!" Chooch said and patted Luno on the back, then helped him up off the floor.

"I look forward to studying a member of the Reptilicon species in close proximity without the possibility of death," said Clive, pecking at his device.

"Are you sure dis ees good idea, Mr. Z?" Roog asked.

Geo waved away any doubt. "Of *course!*" he said, and marched ahead with the others.

"So now that Vlactron has been defeated and we have the Golden Anchovy"—Luno turned to Roog—"everything can go back to normal, *right?*"

Roog sighed and wearily shook his head, then said that the Golden Anchovy was power. Solaro used its power to do *good* things with it, but the same power could be used to destroy planets, enslave people, and even control the universe. Solaro wanted to use it to help *others*, but Vlactron wanted to use it for *himself*.

"And *that's* the difference between a good guy and a bad guy," Luno said. He then turned to Roog and asked, "So this isn't over, *is* it?"

"Eet hass only just begun, boy," Roog said, placing a claw on Luno's shoulder. "Eef anyvun find out dat Golden Anchovy ees not only real, but hass been *found*, dere vill be udders who vill come to take it."

In Elvina's room, Connie and Elvina cheerfully chatted as they put her belongings in a case.

"Will you excuse me, Mrs. Zor—" Elvina caught herself. "I mean *Mom*. I need to get a few things from the other room. I'll be back in a jiffy!"

Elvina gave Connie a little wave as she slipped into the bathroom and quietly locked the door. She rolled back her sleeve and pressed a button on a small device around her wrist.

A hologram of the head of the most vicious, disgusting, and otherworldly lizard-like creature appeared before her in the beam of light emitted from the device.

"Yes?" it asked.

"Vlactron has failed to obtain the Golden Anchovy," Elvina said.

The head grumbled in disappointment.

"I have a plan to get the Anchovy," Elvina assured the creature. "But it may take some time."

A horrible grimace formed on his pasty lips, exposing hundreds of sharp, crooked teeth.

"Time is running out for me as it will for you, my daughter," he said, "if you do not obtain the Golden Anchovy soon."

Then he disappeared.

How to Make a
ZORGOOCHI
INTERGALACTIC PIZZA!

The first thing you need to do is gather ingredients for the dough.

1 ½ cups warm water

2 Tbsp sugar

1 envelope active dry yeast (not the quick kind)

2 tsp salt

4 Tbsp olive oil

4 cups flour

Now to prepare the dough.

1. Combine the water, sugar, and yeast packet in a large bowl and let it sit for 10 minutes. Do not drink this!

2. Add the salt and the olive oil. Again, resist the urge to drink!

3. Add 1 cup of flour at a time, using a whisk, fork, or mechanical claw to combine the mixture.

4. After you've added all 4 cups of flour, knead the dough for 5 minutes. If the dough becomes sticky or irritable, add more flour.

5. Drizzle some oil over it, and then place it in a new, clean bowl. This should calm it down.

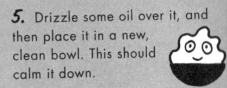

6. Use your hands to spread the oil over the dough as you speak lovingly to it to lull it into a false sense of security.

7. Quickly cover the bowl with plastic wrap or a wet towel and put it in a warm place for about 40 minutes to an hour. You may hear it whimper, but do not uncover it!

Besides, you'll be too busy gathering the toppings:

Nuts and Bolts

Space Octopus

Hot Peppers

Plutonium Pepperoni

Wild Mushrooms

Black, Green, and Blue Olives

Broccoli

Saturnian Sausage

Moon Rocks

8. Uncover the dough and you'll see that it has now nearly doubled in size. Do not be alarmed. Before it can grow or mutate any further, take it out of the bowl and punch it down. This will knock it unconscious, but only for a few minutes, so hurry!

9. Cut the dough in half. Now you have enough for 2 unusually large pizzas. This may be good if you're hungry, but it's a bad move because now you're outnumbered. Get them into the oven as soon as possible or suffer the consequences.

10. Dust your work surface with a thin layer of flour or cornmeal and shape the dough into pizzas. Resist the urge to toss the dough in the air. You have not been properly trained in the famous Zorgoochi Pizza Toss.

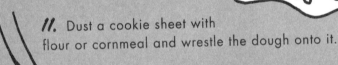

11. Dust a cookie sheet with flour or cornmeal and wrestle the dough onto it.

12. Preheat your oven to 500°F for about 20 minutes.

13. Now, top the pizzas! Spread your sauce, cheese, and toppings evenly over the pizzas. Don't pile on too much or they won't cook properly. If your pizzas eat your toppings, then you clearly haven't punched them down hard enough.

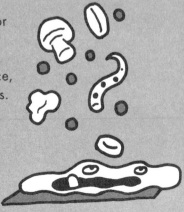

14. If you're on a fire planet like Inferno9, just leave your pizzas on the windowsill and they'll cook in moments. If not, pop them in the oven for about 10 minutes, but check them every 3 to 4 minutes.

A word of caution:
Please be armed while opening the oven door.
The pizzas may have some fight left in them!

When your pizzas appear to be done, take them out, and place them somewhere to cool down, but do not turn your back on them. They may still attack! If you're still alive, slice them up and enjoy!

"Peace, Love, and Pizza!"

—Solaro Zorgoochi

ACKNOWLEDGMENTS

My name may be the only one on the cover of this book, but I cannot take full credit for its creation. Luno, Zorgoochi Intergalactic Pizza, or even the Mezzaluna Galaxy would not exist if it weren't for people whose talent, generosity, and patience helped me write and illustrate my first novel.

I'd like to thank my team at Feiwel and Friends, but first and foremost, my editor, Liz Szabla, who pushed me to push myself to realize my vision for this book. Our many conversations about aliens, robots, and the future of mankind over dill pickles and chopped liver sandwiches were instrumental in helping me realize my vision of the Mezzaluna Galaxy.

Publisher Jean Feiwel provided me with the opportunity to finally fulfill my dream of publishing a science-fiction novel that I would've wanted to read growing up.

Rich Deas inspired me to create images befitting of his wonderful designs. Thanks also to design assistant Anna Booth.

Assistant editor Anna Roberto lovingly looked after my book as it was shepherded through production.

I would also like to thank managing editor Dave Barrett, production manager Nicole Moulaison, and Lucy Del Priore, director of school and library marketing, for whose talents I am so deeply grateful.

I'd also like to thank my confidant, ally, sounding board, and literary agent, Rebecca Sherman of Writers House, for all of her sage advice, hard work, and patience, but mostly for her faith in someone who was primarily known as an author and illustrator of picture books.

I consider myself very fortunate to have people in my life who are not only incredibly talented, but generous with their talents, like Andy Guerdat, Tony DiTerlizzi, and Dave Gordon.

I'd also like to take this opportunity to thank my

wife, Susan, and our children, Michael and Lucy, for their honesty, love, and inspiration, but mostly for making me want to be the best author, illustrator, as well as the best person, I can possibly be.

I hope to get there some day.

Thank you for reading this *Feiwel and Friends* book.
The Friends who made

Zorgoochi Intergalactic Pizza

DELIVERY OF DOOM

possible are:

Jean Feiwel	PUBLISHER
Liz Szabla	EDITOR IN CHIEF
Rich Deas	SENIOR CREATIVE DIRECTOR
Holly West	ASSOCIATE EDITOR
Dave Barrett	EXECUTIVE MANAGING EDITOR
Nicole Liebowitz Moulaison	PRODUCTION MANAGER
Lauren A. Burniac	EDITOR
Anna Roberto	ASSOCIATE EDITOR
Christine Barcellona	ADMINISTRATIVE ASSISTANT

Follow us on Facebook or visit us online at mackids.com.

OUR BOOKS ARE FRIENDS FOR LIFE